AXAR OFTEN

Shadows of the Past

Unmasking the Shadows: The Truth Can't Be Silenced

First edition

This book was professionally typeset on Reedsy.
Find out more at reedsy.com

Contents

The Forgotten Tragedy

The warm glow of the summer evening cast long shadows over the small town, its streets still familiar, despite the years that had passed. Sarah stood outside the coffee shop, the same one they had all hung out at during their high school years. Her heart raced with a mix of nostalgia and nerves as she waited for the others to arrive. It had been years since they'd all seen each other.

The doorbell chimed softly as the first of her old friends arrived.

"Sarah!" Emily's voice broke the silence, her face lighting up with a smile. She wrapped her arms around Sarah in a tight hug. "It's been too long."

"It really has," Sarah replied, her voice warm but with an underlying tension she couldn't shake off. "I can't believe we're all finally back here."

One by one, the others arrived—Alex, Jake, and Mike. The years had changed them all in subtle ways, but the easy banter that had defined their friendship in high school quickly resurfaced.

"I don't know how you convinced me to come back here," Jake said with a smirk, sipping his coffee. "I swore I'd never set foot in this town again."

Alex laughed. "You always say that, but you couldn't resist the chance to relive the glory days, huh?"

"More like to finally get some closure," Mike chimed in, his tone more serious. His words cast a brief silence over the group. The memories of their school days weren't all filled with laughter and teenage antics. There were darker things that had happened—things they hadn't spoken about in years.

As the conversation drifted towards more casual topics, Sarah found herself glancing around the café, her mind wandering back to their high school. She remembered the whispers in the hallways, the tragedies that had unfolded, and the way everyone had tried to move on like nothing had happened. But the truth was, no one had ever really gotten answers. The unsolved crimes from their senior year still lingered in the background, like shadows cast over their memories.

"I've been thinking," Sarah began hesitantly, interrupting a lighthearted exchange between Jake and Alex. "Do you all remember... what happened back then? At school?"

The mood shifted instantly. Emily's smile faded, her fingers tightening around her coffee cup. Alex exchanged a glance with Jake, who raised an eyebrow.

"What exactly are you talking about?" Jake asked cautiously, though the look in his eyes suggested he knew.

"The disappearances," Sarah continued. "The deaths. It's like no one ever really cared about what happened. The police just... stopped investigating. We all moved on, but those families never got closure."

Alex leaned forward, resting his arms on the table. "Sarah, are you suggesting... what? That we look into it?"

"I'm not suggesting anything. I just... can't stop thinking about it lately. How we all just let it go. It's been years, but maybe we're the ones who can finally figure out what really happened."

Mike, who had been quiet for most of the conversation, spoke up. "You really think we can do something about it now? After all this time?"

Sarah hesitated, looking at her friends. "I don't know. But doesn't it bother you? That we never got any answers?"

The table was silent for a moment, the weight of the past settling over them. Finally, Emily spoke, her voice soft but resolute. "It does. It always has."

"Then maybe we owe it to ourselves—and to those families—to at least try," Sarah said, her eyes determined.

Jake sighed, running a hand through his hair. "Well, I guess we've never been the type to back down from a challenge."

Alex grinned. "Besides, it could be fun. You know, like the old days."

Sarah smiled, but there was an unease building in her chest. Something told her that this wasn't going to be anything like the old days.

The next day, they decided to meet at their old high school. It had changed in some ways—new paint, updated windows—but the bones of the building were still the same. As they walked through the familiar hallways, the memories began to flood back, and not all of them were pleasant.

"I swear, this place still smells the same," Jake muttered, wrinkling his nose. "Like a mix of old books and floor cleaner."

Emily chuckled softly, but her eyes darted around the corridors, her usual cheerfulness replaced with a shadow of unease. "You know, I always thought this school had a strange vibe," she said, her voice low as if someone might overhear. "Even when we were here. Something about the way people just...

disappeared."

"I remember the rumors," Alex added, his hands stuffed in his pockets as they walked. "People used to say the school was cursed or something. Every time someone died or went missing, there'd be these insane theories flying around."

"Ghost stories," Sarah said quietly. "But it wasn't just that. Some of those kids never came back. And we never really talked about it."

Mike nodded. "I think that was the scariest part. Everyone was talking about it, but no one was doing anything. The police... they gave up pretty quickly. Just wrote everything off as accidents, or runaway cases." His jaw clenched slightly. "But we all knew better."

They stopped in front of an old bulletin board that was still hanging, though much of the paper had yellowed with age. Sarah traced a finger along the edge of one of the posters, feeling a shiver run down her spine.

"There was always something off about the way the adults handled it," she said. "Like they didn't want to dig too deep. And the students? It was like we were all too scared to say anything."

"Or maybe they knew something we didn't," Jake said, leaning against the wall. "I mean, the things people whispered about... secret meetings, people seeing strange things late at night..."

Emily swallowed hard, her voice barely above a whisper. "I remember hearing that some of the teachers were involved. There was this rumor that one of them... well, you know."

"That was just talk," Alex said, though even he sounded uncertain. "But it's true the teachers acted weird whenever someone mentioned the cases."

"They weren't the only ones," Sarah said. "We all just wanted to forget, to act like none of it happened. And it worked, didn't it? We graduated, moved on with our lives. But those people who disappeared… they never got that chance."

There was a heavy silence as the group stood in the dimly lit hallway, surrounded by the weight of their own memories. The lockers, once filled with books and notes, now stood silent, like tombstones in an empty graveyard. It was as if the school itself remembered everything, holding onto secrets that had long been buried.

"I used to walk through these halls, and I swear, I'd hear things," Emily confessed, her voice trembling slightly. "Like whispers. But whenever I looked around, there was no one there."

Jake snorted, trying to lighten the mood. "Maybe you were just paranoid."

"Maybe," Emily replied, though her face remained pale. "Or maybe we were all ignoring something we shouldn't have."

Sarah turned to face them, her expression serious. "What if those whispers were more than just rumors? What if there's something here that we missed? Something we need to uncover?"

The others exchanged glances, a mixture of apprehension and curiosity growing in their eyes.

"Only one way to find out," Alex said, his tone light, but his eyes betraying a hint of unease.

As they continued walking down the hallway, the air felt heavier, as if the past still lingered there, watching them.

Later that evening, the group gathered at Sarah's house. Her dining table was cluttered with old yearbooks, faded newspaper clippings, and photos from their high school days. The unease from the visit to their school had followed them, hanging over their heads like a dark cloud.

Sarah pulled out an old shoebox from under the table and set it down with a soft thud. "I found this while I was cleaning out the attic last week," she said, carefully opening the lid. Inside were more clippings, but these were even older, yellowed with time.

"What is all this?" Jake asked, leaning forward to peer inside.

"It's from the year everything happened," Sarah explained, her voice steady but low. "I'd kept some of the articles when it was all over. I thought maybe one day I'd want to look back and understand what went wrong, but… I never had the guts until now."

Emily picked up one of the clippings and scanned it quickly. "Student Found Dead Near Woods," she read aloud, her voice barely a whisper. She looked up at the others, her eyes wide. "I forgot about this one. He was in the grade above us."

Sarah nodded. "Tom Weaver. He was found dead a month before the first disappearance."

Mike grabbed another article, his brow furrowing. "And then it just kept happening. A girl in our class went missing, another kid was found near the lake… but no one ever connected the dots."

"Until now," Alex muttered, staring at the pile of articles. "You think these are all connected, don't you?"

Sarah met his gaze. "I do. Look at the dates. First Tom's death, then the disappearances. They all happened within the same few months. And it all started at our school."

Jake shifted in his seat, uncomfortable. "So, what are you saying? That someone from our school was behind this?"

"I'm saying that something happened there. And no one wanted to dig too deep, not back then. But maybe there's more to these cases than we realized."

Mike flipped through another article. "I don't know, Sarah. These cases are cold. If the police couldn't figure it out back then, what makes you think we can?"

"Because we were there," Sarah replied firmly. "We saw things. Maybe we didn't understand them at the time, but we were closer to it than anyone else. And now... now we've got time, and perspective. We can start to piece it together."

Alex leaned back in his chair, arms crossed. "Okay, so where do we start?"

Before Sarah could answer, Emily spoke up. She had been quiet for a while, her eyes fixed on a particular page in an old notebook she had found in the shoebox. "Guys... I think I've found something."

The group leaned in closer as she held up the page. It was an old flyer for a school event, a charity fundraiser. Nothing about it seemed out of the ordinary at first glance, until Emily pointed to the bottom corner of the page.

"Look here," she said, tracing the words with her finger. "This was the last event before Tom died. And it wasn't just a regular event. It was organized by the school administration, the same people who were always around when things went wrong."

Jake raised an eyebrow. "You're saying this flyer is important because...?"

"It's not the flyer," Emily said. "It's what it represents. This event was held the night Tom died. It was one of the few times most of the school faculty and students were all together, in one place. What if something happened that night? What if this is where it all started?"

The room fell silent as the weight of Emily's words sank in.

"I think we need to look into this event," Sarah said quietly, breaking the tension. "We need to figure out who was there, what happened, and why it all started falling apart after that night."

"How are we even supposed to do that?" Mike asked. "We're talking about something that happened years ago. People aren't going to remember every detail."

"Maybe not," Sarah said, flipping through the articles with renewed determination. "But we can start by talking to people who were close to it. Teachers, former students, anyone who might know something. Someone has to remember."

Jake sighed and leaned back in his chair, looking around at the rest of the group. "Alright," he said. "I'm in. But if this gets too weird, I'm out."

"It's already weird," Alex pointed out with a grin. "But I guess that's part of the fun."

Sarah smiled slightly, though the heaviness in her chest remained. "Then let's start with this flyer. I have a feeling it's more important than we realize."

The atmosphere in the room grew tense after Sarah's discovery. Each of them could feel the weight of the past pressing down on them. It wasn't just old newspaper clippings or forgotten rumors anymore—it was real. And the idea of diving back into those dark memories sent a shiver through the group.

"I don't know, Sarah," Mike said, leaning back in his chair and crossing his arms. "Maybe there's a reason all of this was left buried. We were just kids. We don't know what we're getting into."

Sarah's gaze was unwavering. "That's exactly why we need to do this now, Mike. We've spent years pretending this didn't happen. But it *did* happen, and nobody ever cared enough to get to the bottom of it."

Jake looked between the two, a conflicted expression on his face. "I get that, but we're talking about opening up old wounds. We all had our reasons for moving on. What if digging into this makes things worse?"

Emily, who had been silent for most of the conversation, finally spoke up. "Worse than what? Knowing that people we knew, people from our school, either died or vanished without a trace? And we just let it go? I can't stop thinking about it now. I feel like we're the only ones who might be able to figure out what really happened."

Jake shook his head, his voice low. "But why us? We're not detectives. We're just... we're just regular people. What makes you think we'll do any better than the police did?"

"Because we *care*," Sarah said, her voice sharp. "Because we lived it. We knew some of those people. And maybe..." She paused, her eyes dropping to the pile of papers in front of her. "Maybe we're the only ones who remember enough to connect the dots."

Alex, who had been unusually quiet, suddenly leaned forward, his hands resting on the table. "I don't know about the rest of you, but I'm tired of pretending none of this matters. I don't want to wake up ten years from now still wondering what we could've found if we'd just asked the right questions. I say we go for it."

Mike sighed, rubbing his temples. "Alright, let's say we do this. What exactly are we looking for? Are we trying to prove there was some kind of conspiracy? A cover-up?"

Sarah nodded slowly. "Something like that. I don't have all the answers yet, but I think we're on the right track. There were too many loose ends back then, too many things that didn't make sense. And the more I think about it, the more convinced

I am that someone wanted it to stay that way."

Emily looked around the room, her eyes serious. "But if that's true… if someone really *did* want to cover this up, what makes you think they'll just let us dig it all up again? We could be putting ourselves in danger."

A heavy silence fell over the group. They all knew she was right. If there had been something sinister going on all those years ago, there was no guarantee that whoever was responsible wouldn't come after them now.

"That's a risk we're going to have to take," Alex said firmly. "If we don't do this, no one else will. Besides, we've come this far already. There's no turning back now."

Sarah took a deep breath, feeling the weight of the decision settling over her. She knew they were stepping into something dangerous, something they weren't fully prepared for. But she also knew that walking away wasn't an option. Not anymore.

"We don't have to decide everything tonight," she said, her voice softening. "But if we're going to do this, we need to be smart about it. We need to start with the people who were there, people who might remember things that didn't make sense back then."

Mike finally nodded, though reluctance still clouded his face. "Alright. But if things start getting too risky, I'm out."

"Agreed," Jake added. "I'm not looking to become the next headline."

Sarah nodded in agreement, but in the pit of her stomach, she couldn't shake the feeling that they were already in deeper than they realized.

As the group began to pack up for the night, Sarah glanced down at the old flyer Emily had found earlier. The date on it, the names of the people involved—it all felt like pieces of a puzzle that had been waiting for them to solve. And now, they had no choice but to see it through.

Just as they were about to leave, a sudden loud knock echoed through the front door. The group froze, exchanging nervous glances.

"Who could that be this late?" Alex muttered.

Sarah's heart raced as she slowly moved toward the door, her hand trembling slightly as she reached for the doorknob. When she opened it, there was no one there. But something caught her eye—a folded piece of paper, placed carefully on the doorstep.

She picked it up, her pulse quickening. As she unfolded the note, her stomach dropped. The message was simple, written in jagged, hurried handwriting:

Stay out of the past, or you'll regret it.

Sarah stared at the note in her hands, her heart pounding in her chest. The others crowded around her, their faces filled with a mix of curiosity and fear. The threatening message had struck a nerve, instantly changing the tone of the evening.

"What the hell?" Jake whispered, leaning in to read the note over Sarah's shoulder. "Who would leave something like this?"

"Someone who doesn't want us poking around," Mike said grimly, glancing nervously at the dark street outside. "This just got real."

Alex reached for the note, studying it closely. "The handwriting looks rushed, like they didn't have time to be careful. But why leave it here, on your doorstep?"

Sarah shook her head, folding the note and putting it in her pocket. "I don't know, but someone clearly knows we've started looking into the old cases. This means we're on the right track."

"Or it means we're being watched," Emily added quietly, her

face pale. She had been the most hesitant about digging into the past, and now her anxiety was visible. "What if this isn't just a scare tactic? What if they're serious?"

"They probably are," Alex replied, though his voice held a trace of excitement. "But that doesn't mean we stop. In fact, this is exactly why we need to keep going. Whoever's behind this is scared of what we might find."

Jake frowned, looking uneasy. "Or they're confident we'll back off. I'm not exactly in the mood to end up on the missing persons list."

"I get it," Sarah said, her voice firm. "But think about it. We've only just started and someone's already trying to intimidate us. That means we're getting close to something—something they don't want us to know."

"She's right," Mike agreed, though reluctantly. "This means there's more to the story. And it means someone has been keeping an eye on this town all these years. Maybe the crimes weren't just random. Maybe someone's still out there, covering up the truth."

Emily looked at him sharply. "And we're supposed to do what? Keep pushing until we're all in danger?"

"We're already in danger," Sarah said, her voice soft but determined. "But we can't stop now. If someone's still watching us, we need to figure out who it is. And more importantly, *why*."

Alex rubbed the back of his neck. "Alright, but we need to be careful. This isn't some harmless investigation. Clearly, someone's taking it personally."

Sarah nodded, her mind already racing. "We'll be smart about it. We won't confront anyone yet, but we'll keep digging. We'll start with the fundraiser event. There must be something we missed."

Jake let out a long sigh. "Fine. I'm in, but I don't like where this is going. If things get too crazy, I'm bailing."

"We all will," Sarah assured him, though deep down she wasn't sure they would. Once they started down this path, it felt like they were already too far in to turn back.

As they gathered their things and prepared to leave, Emily hesitated by the door. "What if this note is just the beginning? What if things get worse?"

Sarah looked at her friend, trying to sound confident even though her heart was still racing. "Then we deal with it when it comes. But for now, we stick together. We're stronger as a group."

Emily gave a reluctant nod, though fear still flickered in her eyes. As the others filed out the door, Sarah lingered behind for a moment, her gaze drifting back to the note she had tucked away in her pocket. The words echoed in her mind: *Stay out of the past, or you'll regret it.*

A cold shiver ran down her spine, but she shook it off. She wasn't about to let fear stop them—not when they were so close to discovering the truth. Whoever had left that note had made a mistake. They had underestimated her and her friends. And now, she was more determined than ever to figure out what really happened all those years ago.

As she stepped outside, locking the door behind her, Sarah knew that whatever came next, there was no turning back. The mystery they had only just begun to unravel was far more dangerous than they had imagined. But they had started this, and she wasn't going to walk away now.

The game had just begun.

Beneath the Surface

The following day, Sarah and the group decided to take their investigation to the next level. If they were going to solve the mystery that had haunted their school for so long, they needed real evidence, something solid that could point them in the right direction. And that meant looking where no one else had before—the school's old archives.

"This is insane," Jake muttered as they approached the school late in the afternoon. "We're really going to break into the place, aren't we?"

"It's not breaking in," Sarah corrected, though her voice lacked confidence. "The building's still open for staff during renovations. No one will notice a few extra people wandering around. We'll just slip in and head for the basement. That's where they keep the old files."

Alex chuckled. "Right, 'not breaking in.' Just casual trespassing."

Emily, walking close to Sarah, glanced nervously at the darkening sky. "I still think this is a bad idea. If we get caught—"

"We won't get caught," Sarah interrupted firmly. "We're in and out. Quick and quiet."

They reached the school, and just as Sarah had said, the front doors were unlocked. The school was quiet, eerily so, as they slipped inside. The familiar smell of old linoleum and the hum of the building's dim lights filled the space, sending a wave of nostalgia over them, though it was far from comforting now.

"We're really doing this," Mike muttered, glancing around the empty halls.

"Keep moving," Sarah said, leading the way toward the stairwell. "The files should be in the basement. If there's anything about the disappearances or the deaths, it's going to be down there."

They descended the stairs quickly, their footsteps echoing off the cold stone walls. The basement was rarely used, mostly for storage. It was the kind of place students avoided back when they were in school, and even now, it felt unsettling.

When they reached the bottom of the stairs, the basement was dimly lit by flickering fluorescent lights. Rows of old filing cabinets, stacked haphazardly, filled the room.

"Well, here we are," Jake said, running a hand along one of the rusting cabinets. "Hope you're all ready for some thrilling paperwork."

Sarah ignored him and went straight to work, opening the first filing cabinet. It creaked loudly, the metal groaning as she tugged at it. Inside were folders—hundreds of them, thick with years of forgotten reports, student records, and event schedules.

"Start looking," Sarah ordered. "We're searching for anything connected to the crimes. Names of victims, reports, meetings—anything that seems suspicious."

They spread out across the room, each of them rifling through the dusty folders. It was slow, tedious work, but after about half an hour, Alex let out a low whistle.

"Guys," he called out, holding up a thick file. "I think I found something."

The others quickly gathered around as Alex flipped open the file. Inside were reports, marked confidential, from the time of the disappearances. There were student records of the kids who had vanished, but more disturbingly, there were handwritten notes, scribbled in the margins, referencing meetings between the school administration and local police.

"Why would the school have these?" Emily asked, her voice barely above a whisper. "This is police stuff."

"Look at this," Alex pointed out, turning the file toward them. "The police closed the cases almost immediately. And here—these notes make it sound like the school knew more than they let on."

Sarah leaned in, her heart racing. "This is it. This is exactly what we've been looking for. They knew. The school administration knew something was going on, and they covered it up."

Mike frowned, flipping through the pages. "But why? Why cover something like this up?"

"We don't know yet," Sarah said, her mind spinning as she scanned the notes. "But we need to figure it out. We're getting closer."

As they continued reading, a strange pattern began to emerge. There were mentions of a few key staff members who had been involved in meetings with the police—names they all recognized. Teachers and administrators they'd had classes with, people they'd seen almost every day.

One name, in particular, stood out. It was the name of the teacher who had mysteriously left the school right after the last disappearance.

"Ms. Harding," Emily said softly, her eyes widening. "She

was our history teacher. I remember when she left. No one ever said why, but... people talked."

"She's our next lead," Sarah said, closing the file. "We need to find her."

Alex grinned, though the tension was thick in the air. "Looks like we've got our first real clue. Let's see how deep this goes."

As they carefully put the file back, a sudden noise echoed through the basement—a creak, as if someone else was there. They all froze, exchanging worried glances.

"Did you hear that?" Jake whispered, his eyes wide.

Sarah's heart pounded in her chest. "Let's get out of here," she said, her voice barely above a whisper.

They gathered their things quickly and quietly made their way back upstairs, but the feeling of being watched clung to them. They had found what they came for, but Sarah knew that from this point forward, they were no longer just uncovering old files—they were stepping into something far more dangerous.

The next morning, Sarah sat in her living room, the file from the school spread out in front of her. The names, the dates, the cryptic notes from the police—everything was swirling in her mind. The discovery they'd made in the basement of the school had confirmed her worst suspicions. The school administration, and perhaps even some of the local police, had known more about the disappearances and deaths than they had ever let on.

Her phone buzzed, pulling her out of her thoughts. It was a message from Emily.

"Are we meeting up to talk about next steps? This is starting to feel real."

Sarah quickly typed back, *"Yeah, let's meet at my place in an hour. We need to figure out what to do next."*

An hour later, the group was gathered in Sarah's living room, the tension from last night's discovery still lingering in the air. Emily was the first to break the silence.

"I haven't been able to stop thinking about this," she admitted, pulling her knees up to her chest as she sat on the couch. "Ms. Harding… I always thought there was something weird about how she just disappeared after that last student went missing. No one ever explained it."

"She just left," Jake added, leaning against the wall. "No warning, no goodbye. One day she was here, the next she was gone."

Sarah nodded, flipping through the notes they had copied from the school. "It's like the entire town wanted to forget about everything that happened. The school, the police, the teachers—they all pretended like nothing was wrong. But we know better now."

Alex shifted in his chair, his expression tense. "But why? That's what I don't get. Why would they want to cover this up? What's the motive? The police don't just shut down investigations without a reason."

"Exactly," Sarah replied. "There's something bigger going on. It's not just about the kids who disappeared or the ones who died. It's about the people who wanted it all buried."

Mike, who had been unusually quiet, finally spoke up. "Maybe it's not just about them wanting to forget. Maybe someone was *involved*—someone in the school or even in the police department. That would explain why everything was swept under the rug so quickly."

The room fell silent for a moment, each of them considering the weight of Mike's words. The idea that someone they might have known, someone they might have trusted, was involved in the deaths and disappearances felt like a punch to the gut.

"Ms. Harding could be the key," Sarah said, her voice steady. "She was there. She was involved in those meetings between the administration and the police. Maybe she saw something she wasn't supposed to, or maybe she knew too much."

"But how do we find her?" Emily asked, frowning. "It's been years since she left. She could be anywhere."

"I did some digging last night," Sarah admitted, holding up her phone. "She's still in the state, living in a small town about an hour away. I think we should go talk to her."

Jake raised an eyebrow. "Talk to her? What makes you think she's just going to tell us anything? If she left because of all this, she's probably not eager to relive it."

Sarah sighed. "I know, but we don't have a choice. If anyone knows what happened back then, it's her. We need to find out what she remembers, what she saw. Maybe she's been carrying this weight for years and wants to get it off her chest."

Emily bit her lip, looking anxious. "But what if she doesn't want to talk? Or worse—what if she's part of the cover-up?"

"That's a risk we'll have to take," Sarah said firmly. "I don't think she's involved. I think she was scared, and that's why she left. But if we're going to find out the truth, we need to ask her directly."

The room went quiet again as everyone considered the plan. Finally, Mike nodded. "Alright. We'll talk to her. But we need to be careful. If someone's already left us a warning, it means they know we're getting closer."

"And they won't hesitate to stop us," Alex added grimly.

Sarah looked around the room at her friends, seeing the worry etched on their faces, but also the determination. They had all agreed to reopen these old wounds, and now, there was no going back. The truth was out there, buried beneath layers of lies and fear, and they were the ones who had to bring it to light.

"We leave tomorrow morning," Sarah said, her voice steady despite the fear gnawing at her. "We'll find Ms. Harding, and we'll get some answers."

Jake let out a long breath, running a hand through his hair. "I hope you know what you're doing, Sarah. Because this is getting a lot darker than I expected."

Sarah looked at him, her eyes serious. "I know. But if we don't do this, no one else will."

As the group began to disperse, Sarah lingered in the living room, staring at the stack of notes and files on the table. She could feel it—this was only the beginning. Whatever secrets the town had buried, they were getting closer to uncovering them. But with every step forward, the danger grew, and she knew the hardest part was still ahead.

As she turned off the lights and headed to bed, Sarah couldn't shake the feeling that reopening this old wound might come at a greater cost than any of them were ready for.

The next day, the group drove to the small town where Ms. Harding now lived. As they pulled up to her modest house, the nervous energy in the car was palpable. Sarah's grip tightened on the steering wheel as she parked, her mind racing with the questions she wanted to ask. If anyone knew the truth about what had happened all those years ago, it was Ms. Harding.

"Ready?" Alex asked from the passenger seat, though he didn't sound entirely sure himself.

Sarah nodded, though her stomach churned with uncertainty. "Let's do this."

The group approached the house and knocked on the door. After a few moments, they heard footsteps from inside. The door creaked open, and there stood Ms. Harding, older now, but still recognizable. Her sharp eyes scanned the group with curiosity and, perhaps, a flicker of recognition.

"Can I help you?" she asked, her tone guarded.

"Ms. Harding, we were students at the high school," Sarah began, her voice steady despite the knot in her throat. "We're looking into what happened years ago—when the students started disappearing."

Ms. Harding's face stiffened. Her hand tightened on the doorframe, and for a moment, Sarah thought she might slam the door shut. Instead, the former teacher sighed and stepped aside.

"You'd better come in."

The living room was small and cozy, a stark contrast to the tension hanging in the air. The group sat down awkwardly, their eyes on Ms. Harding as she slowly lowered herself into a chair across from them.

"So, you're digging up old graves," Ms. Harding said bluntly. "What exactly do you want from me?"

"We think you might know something about the disappearances," Sarah said, her voice calm but determined. "Your name came up in the school's records—those meetings between the administration and the police. You left the school right after the last student went missing. We need to know why."

Ms. Harding's eyes darkened. She didn't speak for a long time, and when she finally did, her voice was quiet but filled with an old pain.

"You don't know what you're asking," she said. "There are things about that time that you can't imagine. I left because I had to. For my own safety."

"What do you mean?" Jake asked, leaning forward. "What happened back then?"

Ms. Harding's gaze flickered to him, then back to Sarah. "The school... it wasn't just a place for learning. It became something else, something dark. Those students didn't just disappear. They were taken."

"Taken?" Emily's voice trembled. "By who?"

Ms. Harding shook her head. "I don't know all the details. I wish I did. But what I do know is that there were people involved—people with power, people who could make things disappear, including the students. The police were in on it. They covered it up, made sure the cases went cold. And the school... the school was at the center of it all."

Sarah felt her pulse quicken. "Why didn't you tell anyone?"

Ms. Harding let out a bitter laugh. "Tell who? The police? They were part of the cover-up. The school board? They were too scared or too complicit to do anything. I tried to push back, tried to ask questions, and that's when the threats started. They made it clear I needed to leave if I wanted to stay alive."

The room was silent as the group absorbed her words. It was worse than any of them had imagined.

"Do you have any proof?" Mike asked carefully.

Ms. Harding hesitated, then stood up slowly. "I don't have much. But there's something I kept. Something I couldn't bring myself to throw away." She disappeared down the hallway, and moments later, returned with a small, tattered journal in her hands.

"This belonged to one of the students who went missing," she said, holding it out to Sarah. "I found it in their locker after they disappeared. I never told anyone about it. I was too scared.

But maybe it can help you now."

Sarah took the journal with trembling hands. It was worn, the pages yellowed with age, but the writing inside was still legible. The student had written about strange things happening around the school—people watching them, whispers of secret meetings, and a sense of dread that seemed to follow them everywhere.

"There's not much in there," Ms. Harding said softly. "But it might be enough to point you in the right direction."

Sarah flipped through the journal, her heart pounding as she read the final entry. It was short, scribbled hastily as if the student had been in a hurry.

"I'm being followed. I think they know I've been asking questions. I don't know what to do. If anything happens to me, tell someone. Tell them it wasn't an accident."

Sarah's hands shook as she closed the journal. The student had known something—something that had gotten them killed.

"Thank you," Sarah said, her voice barely above a whisper. "This... this could be what we need."

Ms. Harding's eyes were filled with sorrow. "Be careful," she warned. "The people behind this... they won't stop at threats. If they know you're getting close to the truth, they'll come for you, just like they came for me."

The group stood to leave, the weight of the journal heavy in Sarah's hands. As they walked out the door, the realization hit them: they were no longer just uncovering a mystery. They were walking straight into a danger far more real than they had anticipated.

The drive back from Ms. Harding's house was heavy with silence. Sarah clutched the journal tightly in her lap, the weight of its contents pressing down on her mind. They had expected to find more pieces to the puzzle, but what they had uncovered went far beyond what any of them had imagined. The reality that students had been deliberately taken—and that there had been a coordinated cover-up—felt too big, too dark to fully comprehend.

"Taken," Jake muttered, breaking the silence, his eyes staring blankly at the road ahead. "I still can't wrap my head around it. Who does something like that?"

"And why?" Emily added quietly from the back seat. "What could they have wanted with those kids? We've gone from disappearances to... what? A kidnapping ring?"

"Maybe worse," Mike said grimly, his arms crossed over his chest. "We don't know the full story yet, but it's clear these kids were a part of something bigger. And whatever it was, it's been buried deep for years."

Sarah's grip tightened on the journal, her knuckles white. "Ms. Harding was terrified. She wasn't exaggerating about the threats. If they came for her after she started asking questions, they won't hesitate to come after us. Especially now."

"We're already in it," Alex said, glancing at her. "They know we're digging. That note on your doorstep was the first warning, and it won't be the last."

As they pulled up to Sarah's house, the group sat in the car for a moment, the air thick with anxiety. None of them wanted to admit it, but they could feel it—the growing sense of dread, the realization that they were no longer just investigating a mystery but were actively putting themselves in danger.

Sarah finally broke the silence. "We need to go through this journal more carefully," she said. "There's got to be something in here that points us in the right direction. A name, a place—anything that can lead us to whoever's responsible."

Inside the house, they gathered around the kitchen table, the journal open in front of them. The entries were scattered and brief, but they painted a haunting picture of the student's growing fear. The final entries mentioned being followed, overhearing conversations between teachers and administrators, and vague hints of something called "The Project."

"The Project?" Jake raised an eyebrow as he read the passage aloud. "What do you think that is?"

"I don't know," Sarah admitted. "But it sounds like something the administration was involved in. And it clearly scared this student enough to write it down. Maybe that's what they were trying to hide."

Emily's eyes widened. "Could this be what Ms. Harding was talking about? Something that the school was involved in? What if this 'Project' is the key to everything?"

"Whatever it is, it got these kids killed," Mike said flatly, his voice hard. "If we're going to keep digging, we need to be ready for whatever comes next. These people play dirty, and they're not going to let us uncover the truth without a fight."

Alex leaned back in his chair, running a hand through his hair. "So, what's our next move? Do we try to find more about this Project? Or do we focus on finding out who else was involved in the cover-up?"

Before Sarah could answer, a loud *thud* echoed from outside, making everyone jump. The sound was followed by the unmistakable crunch of footsteps on the gravel driveway.

"What was that?" Emily whispered, her face pale.

Sarah's heart raced as she moved toward the window, peeking out through the curtain. Her blood ran cold when she saw what was lying on the front porch—a dead bird, its wings sprawled out unnaturally, a clear sign that it hadn't just died of natural causes.

She pulled the door open cautiously, her pulse pounding in her ears. There, next to the bird, was another note, folded and placed neatly beside the body.

She knelt down and picked it up with trembling fingers. The handwriting was different from the first note—this time, it was bold and precise, almost eerily neat.

"This is your second warning. Drop it, or more than birds will die."

Sarah felt her stomach twist. She turned to the group, her face pale as she handed the note to Alex.

"They're watching us," she said, her voice shaky. "They know what we're doing. And they're not going to stop until we back off."

Mike's jaw clenched as he read the note. "So what do we do now? Back off?"

"No," Sarah said, her voice firmer than she felt inside. "We can't stop. We're close—closer than anyone's ever been. That's why they're threatening us. They want us to be scared. But if we back down now, everything we've uncovered will stay buried forever."

Jake stared at her incredulously. "You're saying we just ignore the threat? We could end up like those kids who disappeared, Sarah. This isn't a game."

"I know it's not," Sarah snapped, her frustration spilling over. "But if we don't figure this out, then they win. And more people could get hurt. We have to keep going, but we have to be smart about it."

Emily was shaking, her eyes wide. "How are we supposed to be smart when we don't even know who's behind this? We don't know who we're dealing with."

"We'll figure it out," Sarah said, though doubt gnawed at her. "We have to."

Alex put the note down and stood up. "Whatever happens, we need to stay together. They're trying to scare us into splitting up, into giving up. But we're stronger if we stick together and keep moving forward."

The group exchanged uneasy glances, but no one argued. They all knew the risks, and despite the fear gnawing at them, they had come too far to stop now.

"Let's get some rest," Sarah said finally. "We'll go through the journal again tomorrow and see if we missed anything about this 'Project.' And from now on, we keep an eye out. If they're watching us, we'll be watching back."

As the group dispersed, Sarah lingered at the table, staring down at the journal. She could feel the weight of the dead bird and the threat behind it pressing on her mind. She had wanted to uncover the truth for so long, but now that they were deep into it, she couldn't shake the feeling that the truth might be more dangerous than any of them were ready for.

The next morning, the air in Sarah's house was thick with tension. No one had slept well after the discovery of the dead bird and the menacing note left on the porch. The realization that someone was watching them, tracking their every move, had hit them all hard.

"I hate this," Emily said as she nervously paced around the kitchen, her arms wrapped tightly around herself. "I feel like we're being hunted."

"We're not hunted," Alex said, though his voice lacked conviction. "We're just... being watched. There's a difference."

"Yeah, great," Jake muttered, staring at the note on the table. "That's supposed to make us feel better?"

Sarah had been quiet all morning, her eyes constantly flicking toward the window, scanning the street for any sign of movement. The journal sat in front of her, but her mind was elsewhere, racing with thoughts of the danger they were facing.

"We have to be smarter about this," she finally said, breaking the silence. "We know they're watching us, and we know they don't want us digging deeper. That means we're close to something. Something big."

"Or it means we're walking straight into a trap," Mike said, his arms crossed as he leaned against the wall. "They're not going to stop with warnings. They're trying to push us to the edge, and when we cross that line, it's over."

"We won't give them the chance," Sarah replied, her voice firm but her hands trembling slightly. "We're careful from here on out. No more late-night meetings at the school or random drives to confront people. We need to stay under the radar."

Jake sighed and leaned forward, rubbing his temples. "So, what's the plan? We can't just sit around waiting for them to strike again."

"We need more information about this 'Project,'" Sarah said, flipping open the journal to the pages where the student had mentioned it. "This was something the school was involved in, something that scared the students enough to write about it. We need to figure out what it was—and who was behind it."

"But we don't have any other leads," Emily said, her voice full of frustration. "We've hit a wall. Ms. Harding gave us the journal, but it's not enough."

"Then we make new leads," Alex said, standing up. "If the school was involved, there has to be a paper trail. Old records, documents, something that mentions this 'Project.' We just need to find out where they kept it."

Sarah's eyes lit up. "The archives. When we were down there looking at the old files, we barely scratched the surface. There could be more—something we missed."

Jake groaned. "You want us to go back *there*? After everything that's happened?"

"We'll be smarter this time," Sarah insisted. "We'll go during the day, when there's less chance of someone catching us. We won't be there long—just enough to see if there's anything we overlooked."

Mike nodded reluctantly. "Alright, but we go in, we look, and we get out. If anything seems off, we leave. No more risks."

"Agreed," Sarah said, her heart pounding with both fear and anticipation. "We'll head over this afternoon. Just... stay alert."

The hours before they left passed slowly, each of them on edge, jumping at every noise or shadow outside the windows. By the time they piled into the car, the weight of what they were doing felt heavier than ever.

As they approached the school, Sarah's stomach twisted with anxiety. The building looked more imposing now, its familiar walls filled with secrets they had yet to uncover. They parked down the street and entered through the back, slipping unnoticed through the halls.

The basement was as dark and musty as it had been the last time, the filing cabinets still looming like silent sentinels. The group moved quickly, spreading out and digging through folders and boxes, searching for anything that could give them more information about "The Project."

"Here," Alex whispered suddenly, holding up a folder labeled **"Special Initiatives 1995"**.

Sarah rushed over, her heart pounding. As they opened the folder, a series of documents spilled out—meeting minutes, memos, and correspondence between school administrators and unknown third parties.

"Look at this," Emily said, pointing to one of the memos. It was a typed note from the school principal at the time, discussing a program that had been initiated for "select students." The memo was vague, but it mentioned that the project was designed to "benefit" students in ways that were never publicly disclosed.

"'Select students,'" Jake muttered, reading over her shoulder. "That doesn't sound good."

"They were experimenting on them," Mike said grimly. "Or using them for something—something they couldn't let anyone else know about."

Sarah flipped through more papers, her eyes narrowing as she found a list of names. It was short—only five names—but they were familiar. Two of them belonged to the students who had disappeared all those years ago.

"This is it," Sarah said, her voice shaking. "They were targeted. These kids were chosen for whatever this 'Project' was. And then they vanished."

"But why?" Alex asked, scanning the papers. "What was the purpose of all this?"

Before anyone could answer, a loud *clang* echoed through the basement. The sound of footsteps—heavy, deliberate—approached from the far end of the hallway.

"Someone's here," Jake whispered, his face pale.

"Go," Sarah hissed, grabbing the papers and shoving them into her bag. "Now."

They bolted for the stairs, their hearts racing as they heard the footsteps growing louder behind them. Sarah's breath caught in her throat as they sprinted up the steps and burst out into the hallway. Without looking back, they ran through the school and out the back door, the cold air hitting their faces as they escaped into the street.

When they finally stopped, gasping for breath, Sarah turned to the group. Her heart was still pounding, but she knew one thing for sure:

"We're not just uncovering secrets anymore," she said, clutching the bag of documents. "We're exposing a conspiracy. And whoever's behind it—they know we're getting closer."

Secrets in Plain Sight

The group gathered the next morning in Sarah's living room, the folder they had stolen from the school lying open on the coffee table. Tension filled the air as they sifted through the documents, trying to make sense of the cryptic notes, memos, and strange lists. But despite the mountain of paperwork in front of them, they were still missing key pieces of the puzzle.

"None of this explains why those kids were chosen," Jake said, flipping through a stack of old memos. "What was this project supposed to be?"

"Look at this," Sarah said, holding up a sheet of paper. "It's another memo, this time talking about 'experimental education techniques' being used on the students in the program. But it's vague, like they didn't want anyone to know what they were really doing."

"It sounds like they were using the students as guinea pigs," Mike said, his voice hard. "But why? What were they trying to achieve?"

Emily was reading through the list of names, her brow furrowed. "These were regular students, weren't they? Why them? What made them 'select' enough for this?"

As the group debated the meaning of the documents, Sarah's

phone buzzed loudly on the table, making everyone jump. She picked it up and froze when she saw the number on the screen.

"It's Mr. Fletcher," she said, looking at the group. "He was our biology teacher. I haven't heard from him since we graduated."

"Why's he calling now?" Jake asked, raising an eyebrow. "Think he knows what we're doing?"

"I don't know," Sarah admitted, her voice uneasy. "But maybe he knows something."

She hesitated for a moment, then answered the call, putting the phone on speaker so the others could hear.

"Mr. Fletcher?" she said cautiously.

"Sarah," came the gravelly voice on the other end. "I heard you've been asking about the old cases at the school. I need to see you and your friends. We need to talk. It's important."

Sarah's heart skipped a beat. She exchanged nervous glances with the others. "You know about the disappearances?"

"I know more than I should," Mr. Fletcher said. "And if you're smart, you'll meet me today. I can't talk on the phone. Meet me at the park by the old school. One o'clock. I'll explain everything."

Before Sarah could respond, the line went dead.

"That's not ominous at all," Jake said, running a hand through his hair. "Think we should go?"

"He sounded scared," Sarah said, her voice low. "If he knows something, we have to hear him out. This could be the break we need."

"Or it could be a trap," Mike said darkly. "We're getting close to the truth, and that's exactly when people start making bad decisions."

Emily shook her head. "We have no choice. If Mr. Fletcher knows something about the project, he might be able to fill in the blanks. We need answers."

They agreed to meet Mr. Fletcher, though the tension was thick as they left Sarah's house and made their way to the park. The sky was overcast, the cold autumn air biting at their skin as they walked. The park, once a popular hangout spot during their high school years, now felt eerie, as if the weight of their investigation had cast a shadow over everything familiar.

Mr. Fletcher was sitting on a bench under a large oak tree, his face lined with worry. He looked older than they remembered, his hair grayer, his shoulders hunched as if he carried the weight of the secrets he had been keeping for years. As they approached, he looked up, his eyes scanning the group with a mixture of urgency and fear.

"Thank you for coming," he said quietly, glancing around as if making sure no one was watching. "I don't have much time."

"Mr. Fletcher, what do you know about the project?" Sarah asked, sitting down beside him. "We found some documents at the school, but they don't explain everything. Why were those students chosen? What was the project really about?"

He let out a long sigh, his hands trembling slightly. "The project… it was supposed to be an educational initiative, a way to test advanced methods of learning. But that's not what it turned into."

The group leaned in closer, hanging on his every word.

"It started off as a legitimate program," he continued, his voice low. "But somewhere along the way, it changed. The administration… they got involved with outside interests—people with money, power. Those kids weren't just being tested on academically. They were being watched. Monitored. For what? I don't know exactly. But it wasn't for their education. It was for something much darker."

Sarah felt a chill run down her spine. "What happened to the kids? Why did they disappear?"

Mr. Fletcher shook his head, his expression pained. "I don't know for sure. I tried to ask questions when the first student disappeared, but I was told to keep quiet. They threatened me—said I'd lose my job, maybe more if I didn't back off. So, I did. I kept my head down. But I knew something terrible was happening. And when more students went missing, I realized that the project wasn't just an experiment. It was a cover for something bigger."

The group sat in stunned silence. Everything they had suspected was true—and worse.

"Why didn't you come forward?" Emily asked, her voice trembling. "You could have told someone."

"I tried," Mr. Fletcher said, his eyes filled with regret. "But no one would listen. The people behind this... they have power, connections. By the time I realized what was going on, it was too late. The kids were gone, and the school was burying everything."

"We've been digging into this," Mike said, his voice hard. "And now someone's trying to stop us. We've been followed, threatened."

Mr. Fletcher's face paled. "Then you need to stop," he said, his voice urgent. "Whoever's behind this—they won't let you expose them. They'll do whatever it takes to protect their secrets. You're not safe."

"We can't stop," Sarah said, shaking her head. "We're too close. We need to know who's behind this and what happened to those kids."

Mr. Fletcher looked at her with a deep sadness in his eyes. "If you keep going, you might find the truth. But you won't like what you find. And it might cost you more than you're willing to pay."

With that, he stood up, glancing around nervously. "I've told you all I can. Be careful, Sarah. You're in deeper than you realize."

As he walked away, disappearing into the distance, the group sat in stunned silence, the gravity of his words hanging over them. The conspiracy was real, and they were in the middle of it.

Sarah clenched her fists, determination coursing through her. "We have to keep going. No matter what it costs."

The others nodded, though fear flickered in their eyes. They were all thinking the same thing: they had crossed a line, and there was no turning back now.

The walk back from the park was thick with silence, each of them lost in their thoughts. Mr. Fletcher's confession had left a dark cloud hanging over the group. The idea that the school was part of a larger conspiracy, one involving powerful people and sinister motives, felt surreal—like something out of a nightmare they couldn't wake up from. But it was real, and the deeper they dug, the more dangerous it became.

As they reached Sarah's house and gathered once more around the kitchen table, Alex finally broke the silence.

"So, what now? We know the project wasn't just about education. It was some kind of experiment, something that got those kids taken. But we still don't know *who* is behind it or *why.*"

Jake leaned back in his chair, rubbing his temples. "Whoever they are, they have power. And if Mr. Fletcher is right, they've been covering this up for years. That means they have influence in the police, the school system—maybe even the town itself."

Emily's face was pale as she stared at the papers spread across the table. "If they've managed to keep this hidden for so long, it means they're good at it. They could be anywhere. And we might not even know who they are until it's too late."

Sarah sat quietly for a moment, her fingers absentmindedly tracing the edge of the journal they had found. Mr. Fletcher's words echoed in her mind: *You're in deeper than you realize.* He had been terrified—of the people involved, of what would happen if they exposed the truth. But the closer they got, the more determined Sarah became. These people had ruined lives, taken students from their families, and had gotten away with it. No more.

"We start by figuring out who at the school was directly involved," Sarah said, her voice steady but firm. "We know the principal at the time was in on it. He signed off on the project. But he couldn't have done it alone. Someone else must have been pulling the strings."

"Yeah, but how do we figure that out?" Jake asked, frustration clear in his voice. "The principal's long gone, and we don't have names of anyone else who could have been part of this."

"Not yet," Alex added, leaning forward. "But we have the files. We know there were meetings between the school and outside interests. That's where we start. We need to find out who those 'outside interests' were."

Emily frowned. "How? It's not like those meetings were public knowledge. If they were covering this up, they wouldn't have left a paper trail."

"They wouldn't have made it obvious, no," Sarah agreed, "but there's always a trail. We just need to know where to look. Maybe there's something in the town archives, or hidden in plain sight—old newspaper clippings, funding reports. Someone had to pay for this project, and money leaves a trail."

Mike, who had been uncharacteristically quiet, finally spoke up. "What if it wasn't just about money? What if this whole thing is tied to something bigger than the school? Something that stretches beyond the town?"

The group turned to him, surprised by the suggestion. Mike leaned forward, tapping the table with his finger as he continued.

"Think about it. The project wasn't just some small-time thing. The way Fletcher talked about it—it sounded like a large-scale experiment. What if the people behind it weren't just local bigwigs? What if this is connected to something much larger?"

Alex narrowed his eyes. "Like what? Some kind of government thing? A corporation?"

"Maybe," Mike said, his voice steady. "We don't know yet. But Fletcher said there were outside interests. If we find out who was funding the project, we might be able to trace it back to the people pulling the strings."

The group exchanged uneasy glances. The idea that the conspiracy they were unraveling could go beyond their small town, stretching into something much more far-reaching and dangerous, was terrifying. But it also made sense. The way everything had been covered up so efficiently, the power and influence needed to silence an entire town—it had to come from somewhere bigger.

"So, we dig into the funding," Sarah said, nodding slowly. "We find out who was paying for this project and who stood to benefit. That will lead us to the people responsible."

"Great," Jake said sarcastically. "And where exactly do we start looking? It's not like these people left a 'Conspiracy 101' handbook lying around."

Sarah glanced at the pile of documents on the table, her mind racing. "We start with the town archives. If this project was tied to the school, it might have been part of the town's public funding at some point. There could be records there, something that points us in the right direction."

"The town archives?" Emily asked, her voice doubtful. "You really think they'd leave a clue sitting in a public place like that?"

"They probably didn't expect anyone to look," Sarah replied. "People like this—they rely on secrecy, on everyone being too scared or too complacent to dig. But we're not giving up."

Jake sighed and rubbed his eyes. "So, let me get this straight. We're going to sneak into the town archives and hope to find, what? A hidden ledger? A contract with 'Bad Guys Inc.'?"

Alex smirked. "Yeah, sounds about right. But seriously, it's worth a shot. If we find anything in those archives that even hints at funding for this project, it could lead us to the people involved."

"And if we don't?" Jake asked, raising an eyebrow.

"Then we keep digging," Sarah said firmly. "We can't stop now."

The group sat in tense silence for a few moments, the weight of their next steps pressing down on them. They were wading deeper into a conspiracy that stretched far beyond anything they had anticipated, but they had no choice. The truth was out there, and they were the only ones who could uncover it.

Emily glanced nervously at the door. "And what if they're watching us? We've already been followed, threatened. If we go to the archives, they could be waiting."

"We'll be careful," Sarah assured her. "We'll go in pairs, keep a low profile. If anyone's watching, we'll make sure they don't know we're onto them."

Jake sighed again. "This just keeps getting better and better."

"Welcome to the web of lies," Alex muttered. "But we're in it now. Might as well pull the strings and see where they lead."

With that, they began planning their visit to the town archives. There was no turning back now. Every step forward was another step closer to the truth—and to the dangerous people who were determined to keep it hidden.

The group gathered early the next morning outside the town's library, where the archives were stored in a small, seldom-used room in the basement. The town, quiet and peaceful on the surface, seemed almost mocking in its stillness, as if it were hiding the dark secrets that had remained buried for years. Sarah felt the weight of what they were about to do pressing down on her. Every step forward was a step deeper into something none of them fully understood.

"I still think this is a bad idea," Jake muttered as they approached the library entrance. "We're basically asking for trouble at this point."

Sarah shot him a determined look. "If we don't do this, no one will. We need to find out who was behind that project, and the answers are in those records. This is our only shot."

Emily looked around nervously as they walked inside, her eyes scanning the quiet hallways. "It just feels like someone's watching us. Ever since we started this, I can't shake the feeling that we're being followed."

"We probably are," Alex said, trying to sound nonchalant but failing. "But we'll be careful. We're here for information, nothing more."

Inside the library, the air was still, the faint smell of dust and old books filling the space. Sarah led the way to the basement stairs, the wooden floor creaking under their footsteps. As they descended, the dim lighting made the shadows stretch long against the walls, and a chill ran through Sarah's spine. This place held more than just old papers; it felt like it held the weight of forgotten stories, things that people wanted to leave in the past.

The basement was small and cramped, lined with shelves of dusty binders, old newspaper clippings, and yellowed documents. The town archives weren't well-kept, likely because no one had been down here in years. That made it perfect for them—there was little chance they'd be interrupted.

"Alright," Sarah said quietly, "split up and start looking for anything that mentions the school's funding or special programs. Especially anything around the mid-90s. That's when the project started."

The group fanned out, each of them pulling old records and binders from the shelves. The work was slow, the documents filled with mundane details about town budgets and planning meetings. It wasn't long before frustration started to settle in.

"This is like looking for a needle in a haystack," Jake grumbled, tossing an old binder onto a nearby table. "We could be here for days."

"We don't have days," Sarah replied, flipping through a stack of old newspaper clippings. "Just keep looking. There has to be something."

After nearly an hour of searching, it was Alex who finally spoke up, his voice cutting through the tense silence. "Hey, I think I found something."

The others hurried over to him, gathering around the table as Alex carefully laid out a series of old financial records. At first glance, they seemed like standard town budget reports, but as they looked closer, Sarah's eyes widened.

"Look at this," she said, pointing to a line item on the page. "Funding for a 'Special Educational Initiative'—dated 1995. That's the same year the project started at the school."

"And check this out," Alex added, flipping to another page. "The funding didn't come from the town. It came from an outside source—some kind of private foundation. 'Satori Foundation'? I've never heard of it."

"Satori Foundation?" Jake echoed, frowning. "That sounds like some shady corporate front."

"It probably is," Sarah said, her heart racing. "This is it. This foundation must have been behind the project. They funded it, but they stayed in the shadows, using the school as a cover. That's why no one ever found out. They buried the money in official reports like this."

Emily's eyes were wide with realization. "So, the school wasn't just a random target. They were chosen—probably because they were small enough that no one would ask questions."

Mike nodded, his expression dark. "And those kids? They weren't just victims. They were part of an experiment. Whatever this foundation was doing, they were using those students as test subjects."

The group stood in stunned silence, the gravity of what they had uncovered settling in. They had finally found a direct link between the school's project and a mysterious organization that had stayed hidden for years. But the question remained: What exactly was the Satori Foundation, and why had they been experimenting on students?

"We need to find out more about this foundation," Sarah said, her voice steady despite the fear gnawing at her. "If we can figure out who's behind it, we'll know who's responsible for everything that happened."

"How do we do that?" Emily asked. "It's not like we can just Google it. They've clearly gone out of their way to stay hidden."

"We can try," Alex said. "Maybe there's some record of them online. If not, we'll need to dig deeper—old newspapers, corporate filings, anything that can point us in the right direction."

Jake leaned against the table, his expression grim. "But the more we dig, the more dangerous this gets. They've already threatened us once. If they find out we've linked them to the project, they'll come after us."

"They might come after us anyway," Sarah said softly. "But we can't stop now. We've already uncovered too much. We owe it to those kids to find the truth."

The others nodded reluctantly, knowing she was right. The weight of the danger was pressing down on all of them, but they had come too far to turn back now. The Satori Foundation was the key to everything, and they couldn't let fear stop them from uncovering the truth.

As they gathered the documents and prepared to leave, Sarah glanced over her shoulder, feeling that familiar chill creeping up her spine. She had been so focused on the search that she hadn't noticed it before, but now she was sure of it.

They were being watched.

She didn't say anything to the others, not wanting to alarm them, but as they left the basement and stepped back into the daylight, she couldn't shake the feeling that they weren't alone. Someone—or something—was lurking in the shadows, keeping a close eye on their every move.

The past wasn't just a distant memory. It was alive, breathing, and watching. And it wasn't finished with them yet.

The group returned to Sarah's house after their tense visit to the town archives, the discovery of the **Satori Foundation** fresh on their minds. The weight of their findings sat heavily in the air, but something else lingered as well—paranoia. Sarah couldn't shake the feeling that someone had been watching them at the archives. The hairs on the back of her neck had stood up the entire time they were down there, and now, as they sat around the kitchen table, she felt it again.

"We need to find out who's behind this foundation," Alex said, tapping a pen against the table. "But this isn't something we can do on our own. We're out of our depth here. We're dealing with people who've stayed hidden for years, maybe decades."

Emily looked nervous. "So, what do we do? We can't exactly call the police—they might be in on it, too."

"That's true," Mike added. "If we go to anyone local, they'll shut us down before we get anywhere close to the truth."

Sarah stared at the pile of papers on the table, her mind racing. She knew they needed help, but she didn't trust anyone in town. The Satori Foundation had kept this conspiracy hidden for so long, and with the way things were shaping up, it seemed like powerful people were still pulling the strings. Going to the wrong person could put them all in even more danger.

Just as she was about to voice her concerns, there was a sharp knock at the door.

The group froze. Jake immediately tensed up, his eyes darting to the door.

"Who could that be?" he whispered.

"Only one way to find out," Alex muttered, getting up cautiously.

Sarah's heart raced as Alex approached the door. She felt a familiar knot of fear tightening in her stomach. What if it was someone connected to the foundation? Another warning—or worse?

Alex opened the door slowly, peeking outside before stepping back in surprise. "Uh, guys, you might want to see this."

The group rushed over, their nerves on edge. Standing on the porch was a woman in her forties, with sharp, intelligent eyes and a look of urgency. She was dressed in a leather jacket and jeans, looking more like someone on the run than someone who had just knocked politely at their door.

"Who are you?" Sarah asked cautiously, stepping forward.

The woman gave a tight smile, though her eyes were scanning the street as if checking for anyone watching. "Name's Claire. Claire Donovan. I'm a journalist. And I think you've been poking around in the same hornet's nest I have."

"A journalist?" Jake asked, raising an eyebrow. "You know about the project?"

Claire nodded and crossed her arms. "I've been investigating the Satori Foundation for years. I didn't know you kids had stumbled onto it until a couple of days ago. But let me tell you, you're in deep. And you're not the first ones to dig into this."

Sarah's heart skipped a beat. "Wait, you know about the foundation? What do you know?"

Claire stepped inside, closing the door behind her. "Enough to know that you're in danger. The Satori Foundation isn't just some shadowy organization—it's a front for something much bigger. Government experiments, private research, all of it hidden behind the mask of 'education initiatives.' They've been operating for decades, targeting schools and students like yours, using them for their own agenda."

Mike looked skeptical. "How do we know you're not just leading us into a trap?"

Claire's expression softened. "Because I've been trying to expose them for years. I've lost sources, colleagues—good people who got too close. And now it looks like you're getting too close, too. I'm here because I want to help. You've found the connection between the school and the foundation, but that's just the beginning."

Sarah exchanged glances with the others, trying to gauge their reactions. Claire seemed genuine, but after everything they had been through, trust was hard to come by.

"Why come to us now?" Emily asked. "If you've been investigating this for years, why didn't you try to stop the foundation sooner?"

"I've tried," Claire said, her voice tinged with frustration. "But they're good at covering their tracks. Every time I've gotten close, the trail goes cold, or someone gets threatened. I didn't even know about your school until I started hearing whispers about some students asking questions. I've been watching, waiting for the right moment to reach out."

Sarah crossed her arms, her mind whirling with possibilities. "What exactly do you want from us?"

"I want to help you finish what you've started," Claire said, her voice firm. "You've got pieces of the puzzle, and I've got the rest. Together, we might be able to bring these people down. But you need to be prepared for what that means. Once you get closer to the truth, they'll come after you with everything they've got."

"We've already been threatened," Alex said grimly. "We're in this whether we like it or not."

Claire nodded. "Then you need to be smart. The Satori Foundation has allies in places you wouldn't believe. You'll need more than just guts to take them on."

Sarah could feel the tension in the room as everyone weighed Claire's offer. They were all thinking the same thing—could they trust her? But at the same time, they knew they couldn't do this alone. The Satori Foundation was too big, too powerful. They needed someone who had experience, someone who knew how to navigate the web of lies they had stumbled into.

Finally, Sarah spoke. "Okay, we're in. But we're not blindly following anyone. If you want to help, you need to be upfront with us. No secrets, no half-truths. We've already been burned by too many lies."

Claire's lips curved into a small smile. "Fair enough. I'll tell you everything I know. But first, we need to make sure you're safe. The foundation doesn't mess around, and if they've already noticed you, it's only a matter of time before they make another move."

"Safe?" Jake scoffed. "We're past that point, aren't we?"

Claire's face hardened. "Not if I can help it."

The group exchanged glances, the weight of their decision settling in. They had just accepted help from a stranger, but in doing so, they were finally taking the fight to the people who had been hiding in the shadows for years.

"Alright," Sarah said, her voice steady. "What's our next move?"

Claire looked at her, determination flashing in her eyes. "We find out who's pulling the strings at the foundation. And then we expose them for good."

As Claire laid out her plan, Sarah couldn't help but feel a flicker of hope amidst the fear. They had a long road ahead of them, but now they had an ally—one who knew the enemy they were up against. For the first time, it felt like they might have a chance to bring the truth to light. But with every answer, more questions loomed on the horizon, and Sarah knew that the deeper they went, the darker it would get.

This was just the beginning.

The weight of Claire's words hung in the air as the group huddled around the kitchen table, their faces tense and pale. She had laid out the connections between the Satori Foundation and other schools across the country, painting a picture far more disturbing than any of them had anticipated. The foundation wasn't just involved with their town—it was part of a much larger web of experimentation and control, hidden behind the guise of educational programs. And now, they had Claire's knowledge to guide them.

"Alright," Claire said, spreading a series of documents and clippings across the table. "We're going to need to be methodical. We've got the link between the Satori Foundation and your school, but we need proof—something undeniable that can expose them publicly. Without solid evidence, they'll keep dodging accountability like they have for decades."

Jake frowned, leaning over one of the newspaper clippings Claire had brought. "You're saying we need to go deeper? We've already found enough to show something was going on. How much more do we need?"

Claire shook her head, her expression grim. "You need a direct link. These people are experts at hiding their tracks. Funding documents, memos, even testimony from people like Fletcher—it's all circumstantial. They can deny it, cover it up, claim it was a misunderstanding. We need irrefutable evidence. Something that proves beyond a doubt that they were experimenting on students, and that they were doing it for their own gain."

Emily looked pale, her voice shaking. "And how do we find

something like that?"

Claire glanced at Sarah. "We go after the source. There are people who know more than they've let on. People who were directly involved in the project but kept quiet out of fear or self-preservation."

"Like Ms. Harding," Sarah said quietly. "But she's already told us everything she knows."

"There's someone else," Claire said, tapping one of the documents. "I've been tracking the names associated with the foundation, and there's one person who keeps coming up—someone who was involved in overseeing the project at several schools, including yours. His name is **Dr. Malcolm Reed**."

"Dr. Reed?" Mike asked, furrowing his brow. "I don't remember anyone by that name from our school."

"He wasn't part of the school directly," Claire explained. "He was the liaison between the foundation and the schools they targeted. He's the one who made sure everything ran smoothly, that the funding flowed and the experiments stayed under the radar. If we can find him, he might have the proof we need."

"Assuming he'll talk," Alex said, skeptical. "If this guy's been involved from the beginning, what makes you think he'll suddenly spill everything to us?"

Claire's eyes darkened. "Because I've been digging into Reed for years, and I know one thing—he's scared. He's been living under the radar for a while now, trying to stay out of sight. But I've heard whispers that he's not happy with how things ended. He's the kind of man who's too proud to let the foundation cut him loose without a fight. If we push the right buttons, we might get him to talk."

"And where is he?" Sarah asked, her heart pounding with both fear and hope. This felt like their first real lead—their chance to finally take control of the situation.

"Last I heard, he's been staying at a secluded cabin outside of town," Claire said. "I tracked his movements a few weeks ago, but I haven't approached him yet. He's paranoid, and for good reason. If we want to talk to him, we'll need to be careful. He's not the trusting type."

Jake sighed, running a hand through his hair. "Great. So we're just going to roll up to some paranoid scientist's cabin and hope he doesn't shoot us on sight?"

Claire gave a tight smile. "Not exactly. We'll approach carefully, make sure he knows we're not a threat. But we need to move fast. If Reed finds out we're onto him, he could disappear again—and we'll lose our best shot at getting the evidence we need."

Sarah felt a surge of determination. "Then we go. We can't let this chance slip away. If Reed knows something, we have to find out what it is."

Emily, still visibly nervous, nodded slowly. "I don't like this, but we don't have another choice. We have to see this through."

Mike and Alex exchanged glances, both of them uneasy but resolved. "Alright," Alex said. "But we do this carefully. If Reed is dangerous, we don't take any unnecessary risks."

Claire nodded. "Agreed. We'll approach him tomorrow morning. I've already got a plan to get us in. We just need to be prepared for whatever happens next."

As the group began to pack up for the night, preparing for the confrontation ahead, Sarah felt the weight of their decision settle over her like a heavy cloak. They were getting closer to the truth, closer than they had ever been—but that also meant they were getting closer to the people who wanted to keep that truth hidden.

When they left Sarah's house that evening, she stood by the door, watching as the shadows deepened outside. For the first time, she felt like they had a real chance of exposing the foundation for what it was, of finally bringing justice to the students who had been taken. But with that hope came fear—fear that they were walking into something far more dangerous than they had ever anticipated.

As she locked the door and headed upstairs, Sarah couldn't shake the feeling that they were being watched. The shadows seemed to linger too long in the corners, and every creak in the house sent her heart racing. She tried to push the paranoia aside, but it clung to her like a second skin.

The truth was out there, just within their grasp. But the closer they got, the more she realized that uncovering it might cost them everything.

Tomorrow, they would confront Dr. Reed. And whatever happened next, there would be no turning back.

The Unraveling

The next morning dawned cold and gray, the sky heavy with the promise of rain. Sarah, Claire, and the rest of the group gathered at Sarah's house, the tension thick in the air as they prepared to confront Dr. Reed. They all knew that this could be their last chance to uncover the truth behind the Satori Foundation, but there was an unspoken fear that had settled between them. Something felt off, and Sarah couldn't quite shake the feeling that they were walking into a trap.

As they loaded into the car, driving in tense silence toward Reed's secluded cabin, Sarah's mind raced. She had replayed the plan over and over in her head—Claire would approach Reed first, using her connections in investigative journalism to gain his trust. The rest of them would stay hidden, ready to step in if things went south. It wasn't a perfect plan, but it was the best they had.

The car rumbled over the gravel road that led to the cabin, the trees growing denser as they left the main road behind. The isolation of the area only heightened Sarah's unease. No one would hear them if something went wrong.

"Are we sure this is a good idea?" Emily asked from the back seat, her voice trembling slightly. "I mean, we're trusting that Reed's going to talk to us. But what if he won't?"

"He will," Claire said, though her tone was clipped. "He's been on the run for too long. He knows that the only way to protect himself is to expose the truth before the foundation decides he's a loose end. We're his best shot."

Sarah glanced at Claire, catching a brief flicker of something in her eyes. Was it confidence? Or was it something else—something darker?

They pulled up to the cabin, which looked as run-down and isolated as Claire had described. The windows were dark, the wooden porch creaking under the weight of disrepair. Sarah's heart pounded in her chest as she watched Claire step out of the car, adjusting her jacket as she approached the door.

"Wait here," Claire instructed. "If he doesn't want to talk, we leave. Don't force anything."

They all nodded, though the unease in the air was palpable. Sarah's eyes followed Claire as she knocked on the door, her movements careful but deliberate. After a few tense moments, the door creaked open, and a man's face appeared—a man who could only be Dr. Malcolm Reed. His face was pale, lined with worry and exhaustion, as if the weight of years of secrets had finally begun to wear him down.

Claire spoke to him in low tones, her voice too quiet to hear. Reed seemed hesitant, glancing over her shoulder toward the car, but after a moment, he stepped aside, letting her in.

"She's in," Jake muttered. "Now we wait."

The minutes stretched out into what felt like an eternity. The forest around them was eerily quiet, the only sound the occasional rustle of leaves in the wind. Sarah's anxiety grew with each passing second, her mind racing through all the ways this could go wrong.

Then, without warning, the front door of the cabin slammed

open. Claire appeared on the porch, her face flushed with urgency.

"Get in here. Now," she barked, motioning for them to follow.

The group scrambled out of the car and rushed toward the cabin, their hearts pounding with both anticipation and fear. As they entered, Sarah noticed Reed standing in the corner of the small living room, his hands shaking as he clutched a cup of coffee. His eyes darted nervously between them.

"You shouldn't have come," he muttered, his voice hoarse. "You don't understand what you're dealing with."

"That's why we're here," Sarah said, stepping forward. "We know about the Satori Foundation, about the experiments. We need your help, Dr. Reed. You're the only one who can expose them."

Reed shook his head, his gaze darting toward Claire. "It's not that simple. You think you can just waltz in here and get the truth, but there are things you don't know. Things you don't want to know."

"We're not leaving until you tell us," Mike said firmly, standing beside Sarah. "We're in this now, and we need to know everything."

Reed let out a shaky breath, running a hand through his thinning hair. "Fine. But you're not going to like what you hear. The foundation—it wasn't just about the experiments. It was about control. Control over the students, control over the town, control over people like me. They used us all. And when we started asking questions, they silenced us."

"How?" Sarah asked, her voice barely above a whisper.

"They made us disappear," Reed said, his voice hollow. "Not just the students. Anyone who got too close to the truth was erased—my colleagues, researchers, even some of the teachers.

The Satori Foundation has been running this town for years. You think you're here to expose them, but they already know who you are."

Suddenly, the room fell into an uneasy silence. Sarah's heart raced, a cold dread settling in her chest. Something wasn't right.

"What do you mean they know who we are?" Jake asked, his voice thick with suspicion.

Claire's eyes darkened, and she shifted uncomfortably. "It means they've been watching you. Ever since you started digging."

Reed's eyes darted to Claire, his voice trembling. "You didn't tell them, did you? You said—"

Claire cut him off, her voice cold. "I said what I needed to say."

Sarah's stomach twisted as realization hit her like a punch to the gut. She turned to Claire, her voice shaking with anger. "What did you do?"

Claire's face hardened, and the room seemed to close in around them. "I didn't have a choice. You don't understand what the foundation is capable of. I couldn't let you keep going down this path—it's too dangerous. If I hadn't intervened, you would've all been dead by now."

"You sold us out?" Mike shouted, stepping toward her. "After everything we've done?"

"I didn't sell you out," Claire snapped, her voice icy. "I'm trying to save you. You're in way over your heads. You don't know what these people are capable of."

Sarah's heart pounded in her ears as the betrayal washed over her. Claire had been their ally—or at least they had thought she was. But now it was clear: Claire had been working with the foundation all along, manipulating them, leading them deeper into a trap they couldn't escape.

"You're working for them," Sarah whispered, her voice barely audible. "You've been leading us right to them."

Claire's expression was cold, her eyes unreadable. "I'm trying to protect you. The foundation—"

But before she could finish, the sound of approaching footsteps echoed from outside. Heavy, deliberate footsteps.

"Get down!" Reed shouted, panic flashing in his eyes.

The group barely had time to react before the front door burst open, and men in dark suits swarmed into the cabin, their faces hidden behind sunglasses. Sarah's heart raced as she and the others dove for cover, the reality of the betrayal crashing down around them.

They were trapped.

Chaos erupted as the men in dark suits stormed into the cabin. Sarah's heart pounded in her chest, the sound of heavy boots and shouted commands filling the small space. She barely had time to process Claire's betrayal before the men grabbed her and the others, forcing them to the ground. The cold floorboards pressed against her cheek as she tried to steady her breathing, her mind racing.

"Don't move!" one of the men barked, his voice harsh and commanding. "Stay down, or it gets worse."

Sarah could see the fear in her friends' eyes as they lay beside her. Mike, Alex, Emily, and Jake—all of them were helpless, caught in the same trap that Claire had set for them. Sarah's stomach twisted with rage and fear. They had trusted Claire, believed she was their ally, but all along she had been leading them straight into the hands of the Satori Foundation.

She lifted her head slightly, catching a glimpse of Claire standing to the side, her expression unreadable. She wasn't resisting, wasn't pleading on their behalf—she was just watching, as if this had been the plan all along.

One of the men grabbed Sarah by the arm, yanking her to her feet. She gasped in pain but bit back a scream, refusing to show them her fear.

"You've been sticking your noses where they don't belong," the man said coldly, his grip tightening on her arm. "Now you're going to answer for it."

"Let them go," Dr. Reed's shaky voice cut through the chaos. He was still standing in the corner, his hands trembling, but there was a flicker of defiance in his eyes. "They don't know anything. I'll tell you what you want—just leave them out of this."

The man holding Sarah didn't even acknowledge Reed. Instead, he turned to one of his colleagues. "Take him outside."

Two of the men grabbed Reed, dragging him toward the door. He struggled briefly, but it was no use. The last thing Sarah saw was Reed's terrified face as they hauled him out of the cabin, the door slamming shut behind them.

"Where are you taking him?" Sarah demanded, her voice raw with anger. "He hasn't done anything!"

The man holding her sneered. "You're all in deeper than you realize. Dr. Reed knows what happens to people who ask too many questions."

Sarah's mind raced, trying to find a way out, trying to make sense of what was happening. But before she could do anything, Claire stepped forward.

"That's enough," Claire said, her voice low but commanding. "We had a deal."

The man glared at her but didn't release his hold on Sarah.

"You did your part. Now stay out of the way."

Claire's jaw clenched, and for the first time, Sarah saw something crack in her cold exterior. "They're not a threat to you," Claire insisted. "They're just kids. Let them go, and I'll make sure this all disappears."

"You don't call the shots," the man said. "We'll take them in for questioning. After that, it's not up to you."

Claire's eyes flicked to Sarah, and for a split second, Sarah saw something in them—regret, maybe, or guilt. But it was too late for Claire's change of heart to matter. The damage was done, and they were all caught in the web she had spun.

Without warning, a loud bang echoed from outside, followed by shouting. The man gripping Sarah tensed, his attention snapping toward the door. Sarah's heart leapt in her chest. Whatever was happening outside, it was her only chance.

In the moment of distraction, Sarah jerked her arm free from the man's grip. She barely had time to think before she lunged toward the others, pulling Emily and Jake up off the floor. "Run!" she shouted.

Panic surged through the group as they scrambled toward the back of the cabin. The men in suits were distracted by the commotion outside, giving them a brief window to escape. They didn't hesitate.

Sarah pushed open the back door, the cold air hitting her face as they stumbled out into the forest. She didn't know where they were running—only that they had to get away, had to put as much distance between themselves and the cabin as possible.

The forest was thick, the trees towering above them, their branches blocking out most of the daylight. The ground was uneven, the roots and rocks threatening to trip them with every step, but Sarah didn't stop. She couldn't. She could hear the shouts behind them, the men giving chase, but the sounds grew fainter as they ran deeper into the woods.

"Keep going!" Sarah urged, her breath coming in ragged gasps. "Don't stop!"

Emily was crying, her face pale with terror, but she kept running. Jake stayed close to her, his eyes wide with fear but his determination keeping him moving forward. Mike and Alex were ahead, leading the way through the maze of trees.

After what felt like an eternity, they finally slowed, collapsing onto the ground in a small clearing. They were all panting, their faces red with exhaustion and fear.

"Are they still following us?" Emily asked, her voice shaky.

Sarah glanced over her shoulder, scanning the forest for any sign of movement. The woods were silent now, save for the distant rustle of leaves in the wind. "I don't think so," she said, though her heart was still racing. "But we can't stay here. We need to keep moving."

Jake cursed under his breath, running a hand through his hair. "What the hell just happened? Claire—she set us up."

"I don't know what her game is," Sarah said, shaking her head. "But we can't trust her anymore. She's been playing both sides from the start."

"What about Reed?" Mike asked, his voice grim. "They took him. He's probably dead by now."

Sarah's stomach twisted with guilt. Reed had tried to warn them, tried to protect them, and now he was paying the price. But she couldn't think about that now. They had to focus on surviving.

"We need to find somewhere safe," Sarah said. "We can figure out what to do next once we're out of the woods."

They got to their feet, their bodies aching from the frantic escape. As they started moving again, Sarah's mind raced. Everything was falling apart. Claire had betrayed them, Reed was gone, and the men from the Satori Foundation were still out there, hunting them. They were running out of time, and the pieces of the puzzle were slipping through their fingers.

But one thing was clear: they had to keep going. The foundation had gone to great lengths to stop them, which meant they were closer to the truth than ever before. And no matter what happened next, Sarah was determined to see this through to the end.

The truth was within reach—but the cost of uncovering it was growing with every step they took.

They finally found a small, secluded spot deeper in the forest, far enough from the cabin that the group felt somewhat safer. They collapsed onto the ground, catching their breath, their bodies still trembling with fear and exhaustion. The weight of what had just happened was crushing down on them, but there was no time to process it fully. They had to keep moving, keep thinking, if they wanted to survive.

As Sarah sat against a tree, trying to calm her racing heart, Emily spoke up, her voice shaky. "What are we going to do now? We can't go back. We can't go to the police. Claire… she's turned on us."

Jake sighed heavily, rubbing his face in frustration. "We're running out of options. And what the hell was that back there? Claire said she was helping us, but she was working with them the whole time?"

"She was playing us," Alex said bitterly. "Probably from the start. Whatever deal she made with the foundation, we're just collateral damage to her."

Sarah stared at the ground, her mind whirling with thoughts

of Claire, Dr. Reed, and the men in suits who had almost captured them. Everything felt like it was spinning out of control, but there was something else gnawing at her—a feeling she hadn't been able to shake for days.

It was something Reed had said back in the cabin. *They've been running this town for years.* The words echoed in her mind, stirring up memories she had long buried. The way the town had always seemed a little too quiet, a little too perfect. The way certain families held a strange amount of influence. The way her own family had always seemed connected to the school in ways she hadn't questioned before.

Sarah's pulse quickened as the realization hit her like a cold wave. "I need to talk to my dad."

The others looked at her, confusion etched on their faces. "What?" Jake asked, frowning. "Why?"

"My dad…" Sarah hesitated, the pieces starting to fall into place in her mind. "He's been involved with the school for as long as I can remember. He's on the school board. He's always been close to the administration. But there's something else—something I didn't think about until now. My family has ties to the people who funded the school projects, including the ones that happened during the time of the Satori Foundation's experiments."

Mike narrowed his eyes. "Wait, you think your dad knew about the foundation?"

"I don't know," Sarah admitted, her voice tight. "But I can't shake the feeling that there's more to this. He's always been quiet about the school's inner workings, but I thought it was just typical school board stuff. What if he's known all along? What if he's been part of it?"

Emily's eyes widened, her voice filled with worry. "Sarah, if your dad's involved..."

"Then we have to find out," Sarah said firmly, standing up. "If my family has any connection to this, I need to know the truth. I don't care how deep it goes."

"You're going to confront your dad?" Jake asked, incredulous. "After everything we've just been through? What if he's in on it? What if he's part of the cover-up?"

Sarah met his gaze, her face set with determination. "I have to take that chance. He's my father, Jake. If he knows something, I have to believe he'll tell me."

"Sarah," Mike said cautiously, "this could be dangerous. If your dad is connected to the foundation, it might be better to keep him in the dark. If you confront him and he's involved, he could tip them off that we're still digging."

"I don't have a choice," Sarah replied. "We're running out of leads, and if my family has answers, I need to get them. We can't keep running forever. We need real information, something that can help us fight back."

Alex stood up, brushing dirt off his jeans. "Alright, but we go with you. You're not doing this alone. If your dad knows something, we need to be there to back you up."

Sarah nodded, grateful for their support. "Okay. Let's get out of here first. We'll head to my house and figure out the next step."

They made their way out of the forest cautiously, taking back roads and avoiding main streets. Sarah's mind was spinning, her stomach in knots as they approached her house. Her family had always been her safe space, the one constant in her life. But now, doubt crept in, filling her with a sense of betrayal she hadn't expected. The possibility that her own father could be tied to the very conspiracy they were trying to uncover filled her with dread.

When they reached her house, Sarah's heart pounded in her chest. The others stayed outside, hidden behind the trees in case anything went wrong. She took a deep breath and walked up the steps to the front door, her legs trembling. She wasn't sure what she would find, but she had to know.

Inside, the house was quiet, the only sound the ticking of the old clock in the hallway. Her father was in his study, as usual, surrounded by paperwork. He looked up when she entered, a tired smile crossing his face.

"Sarah," he said warmly. "I didn't expect you home so early. Everything okay?"

Sarah's throat tightened, and for a moment, she almost backed out. Almost. But then she remembered everything they had uncovered—the lies, the danger, the betrayal. She had to know if her father was a part of it.

"Dad, we need to talk," she said, her voice tense.

Her father's smile faltered, concern flickering in his eyes. "What's wrong?"

Sarah took a deep breath, steeling herself. "I know about the Satori Foundation."

Her father froze, his face going pale. His eyes darted to the door, then back to her, the concern in his eyes deepening into something darker.

"Sarah," he said quietly, his voice strained. "You don't understand what you're talking about."

"I understand more than you think," Sarah said, stepping forward. "I know about the experiments, the students who disappeared. I know the foundation was involved. And I need to know if you knew. If you were part of it."

Her father's hands shook as he stood up from his desk. "It's not what you think, Sarah. I was trying to protect you. I never wanted you to find out about any of this."

"Find out about what?" Sarah demanded, her voice rising. "That you've been working with the people who hurt those kids? That you've been helping them cover it up?"

"I had no choice!" her father shouted, his voice breaking with desperation. "They control everything, Sarah. The school, the town, the police. I tried to fight them, but they—"

"But they what?" Sarah interrupted, her heart pounding. "They threatened you? They blackmailed you?"

Her father's face crumpled, and he sank back into his chair, defeated. "They said they'd come after you if I didn't cooperate. I couldn't let them hurt you, Sarah. I did what I had to do to keep you safe."

Sarah felt like the ground had been ripped out from under her. Her father—her own flesh and blood—had been part of the very conspiracy she had been fighting to uncover. And worse, he had been complicit in the suffering of so many innocent people, all in the name of protecting her.

Her voice shook as she spoke. "Dad, you could have stopped this. You could have told someone."

Her father's eyes filled with tears. "I couldn't. It was too dangerous. And now… it's too late."

Sarah's chest ached with a mixture of anger and sorrow. The man she had trusted all her life had been part of the very machine that had destroyed so many lives. She didn't know what to say, didn't know if she could forgive him.

But there was no time for forgiveness now.

Sarah stood frozen, staring at her father, his guilt and despair written across his face. The man she had always looked up to, the one who had raised her and kept her safe, was now revealed to be tangled in the very conspiracy she had been risking her life to uncover. A part of her wanted to scream, to lash out at him for his betrayal, but another part of her, the part that understood how deeply the Satori Foundation had sunk its claws into the town, felt the weight of his fear. He had been trying to protect her, but in doing so, he had trapped them both in a web of lies.

"I'm so sorry, Sarah," her father whispered, his voice cracking. "I didn't know how to stop them."

Sarah's chest tightened with anger and sorrow, but before she could respond, a sharp knock echoed through the house. Her father's head snapped toward the door, and Sarah felt a cold chill run down her spine. She knew instantly that whoever was at the door wasn't here for a friendly visit.

"Sarah, get out of here," her father said urgently, standing up so fast his chair tipped over. "They're here for you."

"What do you mean?" Sarah whispered, her heart pounding in her chest. "Who's here?"

But before he could answer, the front door burst open with a loud crash. Sarah's father rushed toward the hallway, blocking the entrance to the study. From where she stood, Sarah could see the men—more of the same dark-suited figures who had stormed Dr. Reed's cabin earlier, their faces grim and their eyes hidden behind dark glasses.

"We need to go," her father said, his voice shaking. "Now."

Sarah didn't need to be told twice. She turned and bolted toward the back door, her breath coming in ragged gasps as she grabbed her phone from the table and ran into the night. Her mind raced as she sprinted through the yard, her feet pounding against the damp grass. She had to get to the others. They were waiting in the trees nearby, and together, they might stand a chance.

As she ran, she heard the sounds of the men pursuing her. The crunch of gravel, the rustle of bushes—everything seemed too close, too fast. They were gaining on her.

"Sarah!" Alex's voice called from up ahead, and she nearly cried out in relief. Her friends emerged from the trees, their eyes wide with panic as they saw her running toward them. "What happened?"

"No time!" Sarah gasped, skidding to a stop in front of them. "We need to move. Now."

Without hesitation, the group started running, darting through the dense woods. The trees closed in around them, their branches twisting like skeletal fingers, but Sarah didn't care. The woods were their only hope, their only chance of losing the men who were chasing them.

The darkness pressed in from all sides, and the only sound was the pounding of their footsteps and the ragged gasps of breath. The ground was uneven, the roots and rocks threatening to trip them with every step, but they kept going. They had no choice.

"Do you think we lost them?" Emily asked breathlessly, her face pale with fear.

"I don't know," Jake replied, glancing over his shoulder. "But we can't stop. Not yet."

Suddenly, a loud crack echoed through the forest—a gunshot. Sarah's heart leapt into her throat as she dove behind a thick tree, pulling Emily down with her. The others followed, scrambling for cover as the sound of more gunshots rang out through the night.

"They're shooting at us!" Mike hissed, his face pale in the moonlight.

Sarah's mind raced. They couldn't stay here. The men were closing in, and there was no telling how many of them there were. They had to keep moving, had to find a way to escape.

"Split up," Sarah whispered urgently. "They can't follow all of us. We meet at the old water tower at the edge of the woods."

"Are you sure?" Alex asked, his voice tight with fear.

"It's the only way," Sarah insisted. "We can't stay together, or they'll catch us all."

With a nod, the group scattered, each of them darting in different directions. Sarah's heart pounded in her chest as she sprinted deeper into the forest, weaving between the trees. The cold night air bit at her skin, and the branches scratched at her arms, but she didn't stop. She couldn't.

The gunshots continued behind her, but they were growing more distant. For a brief, fleeting moment, Sarah allowed herself to believe that she might have a chance—that she might actually escape. But then, as she rounded a large tree, a figure stepped out of the shadows, blocking her path.

The man was tall and imposing, his face hidden by the shadow of his hat. He reached out, grabbing her arm with a steel-like grip. Sarah gasped, trying to pull away, but he was too strong.

"Where do you think you're going?" the man growled, his voice low and menacing.

Sarah struggled, her pulse racing, but his grip only tightened. Panic surged through her as she realized she couldn't break free.

Suddenly, from out of the darkness, a figure charged at the man. It was Jake, his face set in a determined scowl. He slammed into the man, knocking him off balance and loosening his grip on Sarah's arm. She stumbled backward, her heart racing, and without thinking, she grabbed a nearby branch and swung it at the man's head.

The man fell to the ground, dazed but not unconscious. Sarah and Jake didn't wait to see if he would get up. They ran.

"Thanks," Sarah panted as they sprinted through the trees.

"Don't mention it," Jake replied, glancing over his shoulder. "We need to get to the water tower. The others are counting on us."

They kept running, their legs burning with exhaustion, but the sound of pursuit had faded. For now, they had escaped the worst of it, but Sarah knew they weren't safe yet. The men wouldn't stop until they found them.

When they finally reached the old water tower, the others were already there, huddled beneath its rusted frame. Their faces were pale, their bodies trembling from the chase, but they were alive.

"We made it," Emily whispered, relief flooding her voice. "We actually made it."

"For now," Mike said grimly. "But we can't stay here. They'll keep coming."

Sarah nodded, her mind racing. They had to figure out their next move, but for the first time since this nightmare had begun, they were completely out of options. They had no safe place left to run, no allies they could trust.

But one thing was certain: the Satori Foundation had underestimated them. They had survived this long, and Sarah wasn't about to give up now.

As she looked around at her friends, her heart heavy with fear and determination, Sarah made a silent vow. They would find a way to expose the truth, no matter how dangerous it was. They couldn't run forever, but they could fight back.

And when the time came, they would be ready.

The rusted metal of the old water tower loomed above them, casting long shadows in the moonlight. The group huddled together beneath its frame, breathless and exhausted. Their bodies ached from the chase, their nerves raw from the fear that still clung to them like a second skin. Sarah scanned the woods around them, every rustle of leaves making her jump. They had made it this far, but how much longer could they keep running?

"We can't stay here for long," Mike muttered, wiping the sweat from his brow. "They'll figure out where we are eventually."

Sarah nodded, her heart still racing. "I know. But we need to catch our breath, come up with a plan."

Alex, crouching nearby, looked up at Sarah. "Plan? What plan? We've got nothing. No allies, no safe places to go. We're sitting ducks."

"That's not true," Sarah said, though her voice was strained. "We've made it this far, and we know more about the foundation than they think. We still have Dr. Reed's information. If we can just—"

"Dr. Reed is gone!" Jake snapped, his voice harsh with frustration. "He's dead, Sarah. And we don't have any proof. Claire turned on us, and now we're running for our lives. Face it, we're screwed."

The words hung in the air like a dark cloud, and Sarah felt the weight of them settle over her. Jake was right in one sense—they had lost so much, and they were backed into a corner. But she refused to give in to despair. There had to be a way out. There *had* to be.

Emily, who had been quiet since the chase, finally spoke up, her voice trembling. "What do we do? We can't just keep running."

Sarah was about to answer when, suddenly, a noise from the woods made them all freeze. Footsteps—heavy and deliberate—approached from the direction they had come. Sarah's blood turned to ice. The men from the foundation had found them.

"They're here," Alex whispered, his face pale.

Sarah's mind raced. They couldn't outrun them again, not in their condition. But if they stayed, they'd be captured—or worse.

"We split up again," Sarah said, her voice urgent. "It worked before. We scatter, we meet somewhere else."

Jake shook his head. "No. We won't make it this time. They'll catch us. We need a distraction."

Before Sarah could argue, Mike stood up, determination etched across his face. He was breathing heavily, his fists clenched at his sides. "I'll do it."

Everyone turned to him in shock. "What are you talking about?" Sarah demanded. "We're not splitting up. We stay together."

Mike's expression softened, but there was a grim resolve in his eyes. "No, Sarah. We're out of time. If we stay together, they'll catch all of us. But if I lead them away, you'll have a chance. You can get out of here and find a way to stop them."

"Mike, no," Emily pleaded, her voice cracking. "You can't do this."

He gave her a sad smile. "I have to. It's the only way. You guys have to survive. You have to expose them. This is bigger than all of us."

Sarah's heart pounded in her chest. She couldn't let him do this. Mike had been with them from the start, had fought beside them every step of the way. She couldn't let him sacrifice himself now, not after everything they had been through.

But before she could speak, Mike placed a hand on her shoulder, his grip firm. "You know I'm right, Sarah. Someone has to draw them away. I'll buy you enough time to escape."

Tears welled up in Sarah's eyes, but she nodded, her throat too tight to speak. She knew he was right. They didn't have a choice.

"Take care of them," Mike said quietly, his gaze moving to the rest of the group. "And promise me you won't stop. Not until the foundation is exposed."

"We won't stop," Sarah whispered, her voice breaking. "I promise."

Without another word, Mike turned and sprinted into the woods, moving in the direction of the footsteps. His movements were deliberate, loud enough to ensure that the men would hear him and follow.

For a brief moment, there was silence.

Then, as if on cue, shouts erupted from the trees behind them, followed by the sound of footsteps chasing after Mike. Sarah felt a pang of anguish as the noise faded into the distance, knowing that Mike was leading the danger away from them—knowing he might not come back.

"We have to go," Jake said, his voice shaking with emotion. "Now."

The group moved quickly, their bodies numb with exhaustion and fear, but they couldn't stop. Mike had bought them time, and they couldn't waste it. Sarah led the way, her heart heavy with guilt, every step forward feeling like a betrayal of her friend's sacrifice.

As they moved deeper into the woods, the sounds of pursuit grew faint. But the weight of Mike's absence was unbearable. Sarah couldn't stop thinking about him, about how he had turned back to face their enemies alone. He had done it for them, for the chance to expose the truth. But the price was too high.

Hours later, when the group finally stopped to rest, the reality of what had happened began to sink in. They were safe—for now—but they had lost one of their own. Sarah sat on a fallen log, her body aching, her mind racing.

Emily was crying softly, her head resting on Alex's shoulder, while Jake stared off into the distance, his face tight with grief. No one spoke for a long time.

Finally, Sarah stood up, her legs shaky but her resolve unbroken. "Mike didn't do this for nothing," she said quietly, her voice steady despite the tears in her eyes. "He gave us a chance, and we can't waste it. We have to keep going. We have to finish what we started."

The others nodded, their faces grim but determined. They knew what they had to do. They owed it to Mike—and to all the people the foundation had hurt.

"We'll fight," Alex said, his voice low but firm. "For Mike."

"For Mike," Sarah echoed, her heart heavy but her spirit unyielding.

They had lost a friend, but they hadn't lost the battle. The truth was still out there, waiting to be uncovered. And now, more than ever, Sarah was determined to expose the Satori Foundation for what it truly was.

Mike's sacrifice would not be in vain.

The Hunter Becomes the Hunted

The days following Mike's sacrifice felt like a blur. The group had made their way out of the woods, exhausted and hollow, but driven by the promise Sarah had made. The loss weighed on them, but it also fueled their determination. They couldn't let Mike's death be in vain. They had to find a way to turn the tables on the Satori Foundation.

The small house they were now hiding in belonged to an old friend of Alex's family—someone outside of town, far enough from prying eyes. It wasn't much, but it was a safe place for them to regroup, plan, and figure out how to strike back.

"We need to go on the offensive," Jake said one night as they sat around a table covered in maps, documents, and hastily scribbled notes. His eyes were bloodshot, his face gaunt from lack of sleep. "We've been running this whole time, but we know enough now. We need to start hitting them where it hurts."

Alex leaned back in his chair, arms crossed. "And how do you propose we do that? They've got resources, power, and people everywhere. We barely escaped the last time they came after us."

"Jake's right," Sarah said, her voice low but resolute. "We can't keep running. We have to strike. Mike showed us that we need to take risks if we're going to get anywhere. And we have the information. We know about the Satori Foundation's connections. We just need proof."

Emily, sitting in the corner, looked up from her spot, her face still pale but more determined than it had been in days. "We need a plan. If we just charge in, we're dead. But if we hit them strategically, if we expose them to the right people at the right time, they won't be able to cover it up."

Sarah nodded, thinking about everything they had uncovered so far. "The foundation's influence is bigger than we thought, but they're not invincible. They rely on secrecy and fear to keep people in line. If we can break that, they'll start losing control."

"What about Dr. Reed's files?" Alex asked. "We never got a chance to see if he left anything behind. If he was tracking the foundation's movements, there might be something there we can use."

Sarah frowned. "We don't even know if Reed's still alive. And if they found his cabin, they probably cleaned it out."

"Maybe," Jake said, leaning forward. "But they don't know everything. Remember how paranoid Reed was? He wouldn't have kept everything in one place. He knew they were after him. He had to have a backup plan."

Sarah's eyes widened. "You think he hid something?"

"It's possible," Jake said. "We need to find out if there's anything he left behind that we can use—something the foundation didn't get their hands on."

Alex sighed. "Okay, but where do we even start looking? His cabin was ransacked, and we barely made it out alive. If there's something hidden, we're going to need a lead."

Sarah stood up, pacing around the room. She thought about Reed's words, about how desperate he had been to protect what he knew. There had to be something—some clue they had overlooked.

"Reed said they've been running this town for years," Sarah said, her voice growing stronger. "He was part of it, but he tried to get out. Maybe he left something behind that connects the foundation to the school, or to the other places they've targeted. If we can find that, we'll have what we need to expose them."

Emily looked at Sarah, her eyes wide with hope. "You think he left evidence?"

"I think we have to believe that he did," Sarah replied. "And if he did, he would have hidden it somewhere only he knew. Somewhere we wouldn't think to look."

"His family," Jake said suddenly, the idea dawning on him. "Reed never mentioned them directly, but there were hints. He was trying to protect someone. What if he hid the files with them?"

Sarah felt a spark of excitement for the first time in days. "It's possible. If he had family, and he trusted them enough, he might have left something with them in case anything happened to him."

Alex stood up, his face serious. "Then we need to find them. We need to find his family and see if they have the proof we need. But we have to be careful. If the foundation knows we're looking for them, they'll come after us even harder."

"Which is why we need to move fast," Sarah said. "We'll split up again—this time to look for any trace of Reed's family. If they know anything, they're our best chance at getting the evidence we need."

The group agreed, tension still lingering in the air, but there was a sense of purpose now—a glimmer of hope. They weren't just running anymore. They were closing the net, turning the hunt back on the people who had been after them for so long.

Over the next few hours, they worked together, combing through everything they knew about Reed. They searched through old records, piecing together fragments of his past life, looking for connections. It was painstaking work, but eventually, they found something—a small, obscure reference to a property on the outskirts of town, one that had once belonged to Reed's parents.

"This has to be it," Jake said, his voice filled with anticipation. "If he left anything behind, it would be here."

Sarah looked at the others, her heart pounding with both fear and hope. "Then we go. Tonight."

They gathered their things, the weight of the night pressing down on them. There was no turning back now. They were no longer the hunted—they were the hunters. And if Reed had left something behind, something that could bring the foundation down, they would find it.

As they left the small house and made their way toward the property, Sarah felt a renewed sense of determination. They were closing in on the truth, and nothing—not the foundation, not the danger, not even their own fear—would stop them now.

Mike's sacrifice had not been in vain.

They were going to finish what they had started. And this time, they were going to win.

The drive to Dr. Reed's family property was tense, the silence in the car heavy with unspoken fears and determination. The sky was a bruised shade of purple, twilight settling in as they drove further into the outskirts of town, leaving behind the familiar streets for the desolate countryside. The further they drove, the more isolated the landscape became, with stretches of empty fields and thick forests bordering the narrow road.

Sarah gripped the steering wheel tightly, her eyes flicking to the rearview mirror every few minutes. She half-expected to see headlights in the distance, the men from the Satori Foundation closing in on them. But so far, the road behind them was clear. Still, the weight of the danger they were in pressed down on her chest, making it hard to breathe.

"Do you think this place is really going to have anything?" Emily asked quietly from the back seat, her voice laced with anxiety.

"It has to," Jake replied, his gaze fixed on the road ahead. "Reed wouldn't have left us hanging. If there's one thing we know, it's that he was paranoid. He wouldn't have let the foundation get their hands on everything."

"And if the foundation already found this place?" Alex asked, his tone dark.

"Then we'll deal with it," Sarah said firmly, though the knot in her stomach tightened. "But we have to take the chance."

They drove in silence for a few more minutes until the old property came into view. It was a small, run-down house, barely visible from the road, nestled behind a thick line of trees. The house had the eerie look of something forgotten by time, the windows dark, the roof sagging slightly. Overgrown grass and weeds surrounded the structure, and the air around it felt heavy, as if it carried the weight of secrets long buried.

Sarah parked the car a little way down the road, hidden by a dense patch of trees, and they all climbed out, moving cautiously toward the house. The silence was suffocating, the only sound the crunch of their footsteps on the gravel path. Every shadow seemed to hold a threat, every rustle of leaves a sign of danger.

"Stay sharp," Sarah whispered, her voice barely audible. "We don't know who else might be here."

They approached the house slowly, their hearts pounding in their chests. Sarah tried the door, but it was locked. Of course. Reed wouldn't have made it easy. Jake produced a small tool kit from his bag, his fingers working quickly to pick the lock. Within minutes, the door clicked open, and they stepped inside, the air thick with dust and the smell of damp wood.

The inside of the house was sparse, with old furniture covered in sheets and a thin layer of dust coating every surface. It felt abandoned, untouched for years. But they knew better. Somewhere in this place, Dr. Reed had left something behind—something that could bring the Satori Foundation down.

"Let's split up," Sarah said quietly. "Search everywhere. If Reed left something, it could be hidden anywhere."

They moved through the house, their footsteps cautious. Sarah headed for what looked like a study, a small room at the back of the house with old wooden shelves lined with books and papers. The room felt like the kind of place where secrets could be hidden, and Sarah's pulse quickened as she began sifting through the shelves, pulling down old books and checking behind them.

The others spread out through the house. Emily searched the kitchen, while Alex and Jake moved upstairs, looking for anything that seemed out of place. Every creak of the old floorboards set them on edge, every gust of wind outside sounding like a threat. The weight of the task before them pressed down heavily.

As Sarah pulled a particularly old, dusty book from the shelf, something caught her eye. The back panel of the shelf had a small, almost imperceptible crack along the edge, as if it wasn't fully attached. Her heart raced as she reached for the panel, pulling it away carefully.

Behind it, she found a small, metal box. It was old and worn, with no markings on it, but her instincts told her this was what they had been looking for. With trembling fingers, she pried it open.

Inside, there were several documents, photographs, and a small flash drive.

"Guys, I found something," Sarah called out, her voice barely above a whisper as she stared at the contents of the box. She felt a surge of excitement and fear all at once. This could be it. The proof they needed.

The others rushed into the room, gathering around her as she spread the documents and photographs out on the floor. The photos were grainy, but they showed something unmistakable—rows of students in what looked like a clinical setting, each one hooked up to machines, their faces blank, almost vacant.

"Oh my God," Emily breathed, her eyes wide with horror. "They really were experimenting on them."

"These are the kids who disappeared," Jake said, his voice tight with anger. "This is what they were doing to them."

Sarah's hands shook as she picked up the flash drive. "We need to see what's on this. If it's anything like the documents, it could be exactly what we need to expose them."

Alex nodded. "There's a laptop in the car. We'll check it once we're out of here."

But before they could make another move, a loud crash echoed through the house, the front door slamming open. Sarah's heart leapt into her throat as they all froze.

"They're here," Alex whispered, his voice filled with panic.

"Go!" Sarah hissed, grabbing the metal box and shoving it into her bag. "We have to get out of here. Now!"

They bolted for the back door, their footsteps frantic. The sound of men storming into the house grew louder, their shouts echoing through the walls.

As they burst through the back door, sprinting into the woods, Sarah's heart pounded with fear and adrenaline. They had the proof they needed, but the foundation was right on their heels.

Branches whipped at their faces as they ran through the trees, the darkness of the night pressing in on them. The sound of their pursuers grew louder, the men from the foundation determined not to let them escape with what they had found.

"Keep going!" Sarah urged, her breath coming in ragged gasps.

But before they could get far, a figure appeared in front of them, stepping out from behind a tree. It was one of the men in suits, his face twisted into a cold smile.

"Going somewhere?" he sneered, raising a gun.

Panic surged through Sarah as she skidded to a stop, her mind racing. The others stopped behind her, their faces pale with fear.

There was no way out.

But before the man could act, a loud crack echoed through the air—a gunshot. The man staggered backward, his eyes wide with shock before he collapsed to the ground, unmoving.

Sarah whipped around, her eyes wide with disbelief.

Standing there, just beyond the tree line, was a figure she hadn't expected to see.

It was Claire.

The forest was silent in the moments after the gunshot, the echo of the blast fading into the night. The group stared in shock as Claire stepped forward, lowering the smoking gun in her hand. Her face was set in a hard, determined expression, her eyes darting between the group and the body of the man she had just shot.

"Claire?" Sarah whispered, her voice thick with disbelief. "What—what are you doing here?"

Claire tucked the gun into her jacket, her lips pressed into a thin line. "Saving your lives, apparently."

Alex stepped forward, his face tight with anger and confusion. "Saving us? You set us up! You betrayed us back at Reed's cabin. Why should we trust you now?"

"I didn't have a choice back then," Claire snapped, her voice sharp with frustration. "You don't understand what the foundation is capable of. They would have killed all of you if I hadn't intervened. I was trying to protect you by keeping them off your trail. But things have changed."

"Changed how?" Jake demanded, his fists clenched. "How do we know you're not just leading us into another trap?"

Claire looked at him, her gaze steady. "Because I'm here, aren't I? I just killed one of their men. That's not something I can undo. The moment I pulled the trigger, I made my choice. I'm on your side now, whether you like it or not."

Sarah's heart pounded in her chest. Claire had betrayed them once before, and now she was claiming to be on their side again. But the danger they were in was very real, and without her help, they might not make it out alive.

"What do you want?" Sarah asked, her voice low but steady. "Why come back now?"

Claire let out a heavy sigh, her shoulders sagging slightly. "Because I realized I can't run from this anymore. The foundation... they're too powerful. They've been controlling people like me for years, keeping us in line with fear, threats, blackmail. But I'm done being afraid. If you've found what I think you've found, then there's a chance to take them down for good."

"We found evidence," Sarah said cautiously, glancing at the bag that held the documents and flash drive. "But we don't know if it's enough. The foundation still has people everywhere."

"That's why you need me," Claire said, stepping closer. "I know how they work. I know where their weak points are. If you want to expose them, you need to do it strategically—hit them where they can't recover."

"Why should we believe you?" Emily asked, her voice shaking. "You've lied to us before. How do we know this isn't just another game?"

Claire's face softened slightly, a flicker of regret in her eyes. "You're right. I lied. I betrayed your trust, and I won't ask you to forgive me for that. But I'm trying to make things right now. I want to help you take them down. I know how dangerous they are, and I know that if we don't stop them now, they'll keep hurting people—kids, families, anyone who gets in their way."

Sarah stared at Claire, her mind racing. Could they really trust her? After everything that had happened, the betrayal, the danger, the lies—how could they trust her again?

But as much as she wanted to deny it, Sarah knew they needed help. The Satori Foundation was bigger and more powerful than they had ever imagined, and if Claire knew how to hit them where it hurt, they couldn't afford to turn her away.

"Okay," Sarah said finally, her voice steady. "We'll work with you. But if you betray us again, I swear—"

"I won't," Claire interrupted, her eyes meeting Sarah's. "I won't. I'm in this now, for real."

Jake scowled but didn't argue. Alex crossed his arms, still

glaring at Claire, but he didn't object either. The decision had been made.

"Good," Claire said, glancing over her shoulder at the woods. "Because we don't have much time. That gunshot will bring more of them soon, and we need to get out of here."

"Where do we go?" Sarah asked, her heart pounding with both fear and anticipation. "We can't just keep running forever."

"We're not running," Claire replied. "We're going to take the fight to them."

Alex raised an eyebrow. "What do you mean?"

Claire's expression hardened. "The Satori Foundation has a central hub—a location they don't advertise, but it's where they store all their critical data. It's where they control everything from. If we can get there, if we can access their systems, we can expose everything. All the evidence, all their secrets—it'll be out in the open."

"How do we even know this place exists?" Jake asked skeptically.

"Because I've been there," Claire said, her voice low. "It's in a building downtown, disguised as a research lab. They call it the Nexus. If we can get in, we'll find everything we need to bring them down."

Sarah felt a surge of hope, mixed with fear. This was the first real plan they had, a tangible goal they could work toward. But it was also incredibly dangerous. If they failed, if they were caught, it would be over—not just for them, but for anyone who had ever been victimized by the foundation.

"How do we get in?" Sarah asked, her voice steady despite the fear gnawing at her.

Claire gave a grim smile. "Leave that to me. I still have a few contacts on the inside. I can get us access. But once we're in, it's up to you to find the data. We have to move fast, before they realize what we're doing."

The group exchanged nervous glances, but the decision had already been made. They had come too far to turn back now, and Claire's plan was the only one that gave them a real shot at taking down the Satori Foundation.

"Alright," Sarah said, her voice firm. "Let's do this."

Claire nodded. "We'll go tonight. There's no time to waste."

As they started moving through the woods, heading back to the car, Sarah's mind raced with the enormity of what they were about to do. The Satori Foundation had been chasing them for days, controlling their lives from the shadows, and now they were about to strike back.

But as they moved deeper into the darkness, Sarah couldn't shake the feeling that something was still lurking, just out of sight. They were closing in on the truth, but the closer they got, the more dangerous it became.

And with Claire back in the mix, Sarah couldn't help but wonder—was this really the endgame, or was it just another layer of the deception they had been trapped in all along?

For now, there was no time to question it. They had a mission.

And the hunt was about to begin.

The city loomed ahead as they drove in tense silence, the lights of downtown reflecting off the windshield like scattered stars. It felt surreal to be heading back into the heart of everything, after days of hiding, running, and being hunted. But this time, they weren't running anymore. They were headed straight into the belly of the beast—the Nexus.

Claire drove, her hands steady on the wheel, though her eyes darted constantly to the rearview mirror, as if expecting to see the foundation's men tailing them. Sarah sat beside her, her mind racing. The plan was dangerous, almost reckless, but it was their best shot at finally bringing the Satori Foundation down.

Behind them, Alex, Jake, and Emily sat in the backseat, the tension so thick it was almost suffocating. They had spent the last hour going over the plan again and again, trying to anticipate every possible outcome, every variable. But there were still so many unknowns.

"You're sure this will work?" Jake asked, breaking the silence. His voice was low, but there was an edge of fear in it.

"It'll work," Claire replied, her voice firm but quiet. "I've been in the Nexus before. They don't expect anyone to be bold enough to break in. They rely on secrecy and intimidation. Once we're inside, they won't know what hit them."

Sarah turned to her, doubt gnawing at her gut. "But how do we get in? You said you had contacts—what if they're not reliable? What if this is another trap?"

Claire glanced at her, the streetlights casting shadows across her face. "I'm not leading you into another trap. My contact knows what's at stake. They're just as eager to see the foundation fall as we are. Trust me."

Sarah didn't answer. Trusting Claire had cost them dearly once before, and even now, despite everything, she couldn't shake the nagging feeling of unease. But they didn't have a choice. If Claire's plan failed, if the Nexus wasn't what she said it was, they were finished.

As they neared the outskirts of downtown, the high-rise buildings towering above them, Claire took a sharp turn down a side street, pulling into the parking lot of a nondescript office building. It was an unremarkable structure, blending in with the other corporate facades in the area. But Sarah knew that behind its unassuming exterior, the Satori Foundation was hiding its most damning secrets.

"This is it," Claire said, killing the engine. "We're here."

The group piled out of the car, their movements quiet, careful. The streets were mostly empty this late at night, but Sarah couldn't shake the feeling that they were being watched—that at any moment, the foundation's men could appear, ready to end it all.

"You're sure this is the place?" Alex asked, eyeing the building with suspicion. "It looks like every other boring office downtown."

"That's the point," Claire replied, leading them toward a side entrance. "They hide in plain sight. Nobody would think twice about this place. But inside, it's where they store all their critical data, all their research. If we can get into their system, we'll have everything we need."

They followed her to the door, which was locked. Claire pulled out a small keycard, swiping it across the reader. The light on the panel turned green, and the door clicked open.

"Where did you get that?" Emily whispered, her eyes wide.

"I told you," Claire said, pushing the door open. "I have contacts."

They stepped inside, the air cool and sterile. The building was eerily quiet, the faint hum of fluorescent lights buzzing overhead. It felt too calm, too still, as if they had walked into the heart of a sleeping beast.

"Where do we go from here?" Sarah asked, her voice barely above a whisper.

"The server room is on the third floor," Claire replied, glancing down the empty hallway. "That's where we'll find the data. But we need to move fast. Security patrols this place at night, and if they catch us—"

"We know what happens," Jake muttered.

They moved quickly but carefully, keeping to the shadows as they made their way to the stairwell. Every step felt like a risk, every corner they turned a potential ambush. Sarah's heart pounded in her chest, the weight of what they were about to do pressing down on her with every passing second.

When they reached the third floor, Claire led them down a long hallway lined with identical doors, each one locked and silent. Finally, she stopped in front of one door marked "Authorized Personnel Only."

"This is it," Claire whispered, pulling out another keycard. "Once we're inside, we need to download everything we can from their servers. It'll take time, so we'll have to be on high alert."

She swiped the card, and the door clicked open. The room beyond was filled with rows of servers, their lights blinking in the dim glow of the room. The air was cool, almost freezing, and the faint hum of the machines filled the space with an unsettling energy.

"Okay," Claire said, motioning to Sarah and Alex. "Get to work. Download as much as you can. Jake, Emily, keep watch at the door. We can't let anyone sneak up on us."

Sarah and Alex moved to the nearest terminal, plugging in the flash drive they had brought. The screen flickered to life, and Sarah's fingers flew over the keyboard, her heart pounding as the data began to transfer.

"This is it," Alex muttered, his voice filled with awe. "Everything we need."

Sarah glanced at the screen, her breath catching in her throat. It was all there—financial records, experiment logs, communications between high-ranking officials, names of people involved. It was more than they had ever hoped for.

But as the data continued to download, Sarah's sense of triumph was overshadowed by a gnawing feeling of dread. Something wasn't right.

"How much longer?" Jake asked from the doorway, his voice tense.

"Almost there," Sarah replied, her fingers trembling as the progress bar slowly filled. "Just a few more minutes."

Suddenly, the door behind them slammed shut with a loud *bang*. Sarah spun around, her heart leaping into her throat.

Standing in the doorway were two men in dark suits, their faces expressionless, their eyes cold.

"You didn't think it would be that easy, did you?" one of them sneered.

Panic surged through Sarah as she stepped back, her eyes darting between the men and the computer screen. They were so close. They couldn't fail now.

"Run!" Claire shouted, pulling out the gun she had used earlier, aiming it at the men.

Before Sarah could react, the room exploded into chaos. Shots rang out, the sound deafening in the small space. One of the men crumpled to the floor, but the other charged at them, moving too fast for Claire to react.

"Sarah, go!" Claire screamed as she struggled with the man, the two of them grappling near the door.

Sarah didn't hesitate. She grabbed the flash drive from the terminal, her heart racing as she bolted for the door. Alex and Jake followed, their footsteps echoing through the hallway as they sprinted toward the stairwell.

But as they ran, Sarah's mind raced with fear and confusion.

Claire had stayed behind to fight, but why? Was this part of her plan, or had she just sacrificed herself for them?

There was no time to think about it. All that mattered now was getting out alive—with the data.

As they burst through the stairwell door, Sarah knew one thing for certain: they had the proof. But the battle was far from over.

And the Satori Foundation wasn't going to let them escape without a fight.

The stairwell echoed with the sound of their pounding footsteps, every sharp breath and thudding step amplifying the fear coursing through Sarah's veins. She clutched the flash drive tightly in her fist, its contents now their only hope of bringing down the Satori Foundation. The realization that they were mere minutes away from either exposing the truth or losing everything propelled her forward, even as her legs burned from the sprint.

"Keep moving!" Alex shouted from behind her. His voice was tight with panic, but he didn't slow down.

Behind them, Sarah could hear the commotion from the server room—the sound of Claire struggling with the remaining man, the gunshots, the chaos. She didn't know if Claire would make it out alive, but there was no time to think about that now. They had to get out.

As they reached the bottom of the stairwell, Jake yanked open the door to the building's back exit, and they spilled out into the cool night air. The alley was deserted, the narrow path between buildings cloaked in shadow. For a split second, Sarah felt a surge of relief, thinking they had made it.

But then, headlights flashed at the far end of the alley, the roar of an engine shattering the momentary calm.

"They're coming," Jake panted, his voice frantic. "We need to go—now!"

Sarah's heart raced as the car screeched toward them, its dark silhouette unmistakable as one of the foundation's vehicles. She turned on her heel, sprinting down the alley in the opposite direction, her mind screaming at her to move faster. She could hear the others running behind her, their breaths ragged and panicked, but they were out in the open, exposed.

The car roared closer, its tires skidding as it rounded the corner. Sarah's pulse spiked with fear as she spotted a side street up ahead, a narrow gap between two buildings. "This way!" she shouted, veering toward it.

They dashed into the side street just as the car sped past them, the headlights briefly illuminating the alley before the vehicle continued down the main road. For a brief moment, they were hidden in the shadows, safe from view.

"Is everyone okay?" Sarah asked, gasping for breath as she leaned against the brick wall of one of the buildings.

"Yeah," Emily said shakily, clutching her side. "For now."

Jake wiped sweat from his brow, his face pale. "They'll double back. We can't stay here."

"We need to get to the car," Alex said, glancing over his shoulder as if expecting the men in suits to appear at any moment. "It's parked a few blocks away. If we can get there before they find us, we'll have a shot at getting out of the city."

Sarah nodded, pushing herself off the wall. "Let's move."

They stayed low, sticking to the shadows as they wound their way through the maze of side streets and alleyways. The night seemed to stretch on forever, the city lights casting long, eerie shadows across the pavement. Every sound felt like a threat—the distant hum of traffic, the echo of their footsteps on the concrete.

After what felt like an eternity, they reached the spot where Claire had parked the car. It was still there, hidden in a dark corner of a parking lot. Relief washed over Sarah as they approached the vehicle, their breaths coming in ragged gasps.

But as they reached the car, Sarah's relief was shattered by the sound of another engine revving behind them. She spun around, her heart dropping into her stomach.

Another car was speeding toward them, its headlights cutting through the darkness. This one wasn't going to miss them.

"Get in!" Alex yelled, throwing open the driver's door and jumping into the seat.

Sarah, Jake, and Emily scrambled into the car just as the other vehicle screeched to a stop behind them. The men from the foundation spilled out, guns drawn, their expressions cold and merciless.

Alex floored the gas pedal, and the car lurched forward, the tires squealing as they sped out of the parking lot. The foundation's men jumped back into their own car, hot on their heels.

Sarah clutched the seat, her knuckles white as Alex tore down the city streets, weaving through traffic in a desperate attempt to lose their pursuers. Her mind raced, replaying everything that had happened in the Nexus. They had the data. They had the evidence. But now they were in a life-or-death chase, and if they didn't lose the foundation's men soon, none of it would matter.

"They're gaining on us!" Jake shouted from the back seat, glancing out the rear window. The other car was closing the distance, its headlights blinding as it barreled toward them.

"Hang on!" Alex yelled, jerking the wheel to the left and

swerving into a narrow alleyway. The car barely fit, the side mirrors scraping against the brick walls as they sped through the tight space.

For a moment, Sarah thought they might lose their pursuers, but when they emerged from the alley, the foundation's car was right behind them, its engine roaring as it gave chase.

"They're not giving up," Emily said, her voice trembling. "What do we do?"

Sarah's mind raced. They were running out of options. But then, through the haze of fear and exhaustion, an idea sparked. "There's a bridge up ahead," she said, her voice steady despite the chaos around her. "If we can get across it, we might be able to lose them on the other side. But we have to time it right."

Alex nodded, his jaw clenched as he sped toward the bridge. The foundation's car was still on their tail, the distance between them shrinking with every second. The bridge was just up ahead, the lights reflecting off the water below.

"Now!" Sarah shouted as they reached the edge of the bridge.

Alex slammed on the brakes, the tires screeching as the car skidded to a stop. The foundation's car shot past them, barreling onto the bridge at full speed. Before the men could react, Alex threw the car into reverse, backing into a side street and disappearing into the shadows.

The foundation's car raced across the bridge, unaware that they had been outmaneuvered. For the first time since the chase had begun, the group breathed a sigh of relief.

"We did it," Jake gasped, his voice filled with disbelief.

Sarah slumped back in her seat, her heart still racing. They had escaped, but the danger wasn't over. Not yet.

"Let's get out of here," Alex said, pulling the car back onto the main road, but keeping their speed low and steady, blending into the flow of traffic.

As they drove away, leaving the city behind, Sarah's mind was still spinning. They had the data. They had the proof. But now they had to figure out how to use it. The Satori Foundation was powerful, and even with the evidence in their hands, they were up against an enemy that wouldn't stop until it was destroyed—or until it destroyed them.

"We have to be smart about this," Sarah said quietly, staring out the window as the city lights faded into the distance. "We can't just release this on our own. We need help. We need someone who can get this out to the world, someone the foundation can't silence."

"But who?" Emily asked, her voice filled with exhaustion.

"We'll figure it out," Sarah replied, her determination unwavering. "We have to."

As they drove into the night, leaving behind the chaos and danger of the Nexus, Sarah felt a new resolve settle over her. They had escaped, but the fight was far from over. The Satori Foundation was still out there, still dangerous. But now, for the first time, they had the upper hand.

And they weren't going to stop until the foundation was brought to its knees.

The Final Countdown

The night stretched on as they drove through empty roads, leaving the city and its chaos behind. The adrenaline from the escape had worn off, leaving Sarah feeling heavy and exhausted. Yet, despite the exhaustion tugging at her, her mind wouldn't slow down. They had the proof—the flash drive in her bag was their key to bringing down the Satori Foundation—but now they needed a plan.

The car hummed quietly as Alex steered them down a dark, winding road. Emily had fallen asleep in the backseat, her head resting against the window, while Jake stared out into the night, his expression unreadable. The weight of their situation pressed down on them all.

"We need to figure out our next move," Sarah said quietly, breaking the silence. "The foundation will be looking for us, and they won't stop until they track us down. We can't just release this on our own. We need help. We need someone who can protect us and make sure this gets out to the right people."

"Who do we trust?" Alex asked, keeping his eyes on the road. "The foundation has people everywhere. The police, the media… they can cover this up in a heartbeat if we're not careful."

Sarah's stomach twisted. He was right. They had already

seen how far the foundation's influence reached. One wrong move, and everything they had fought for would be erased. The evidence, Mike's sacrifice—it would all mean nothing.

"We need to go public, but not in the way they'd expect," Sarah said, her mind racing as she tried to think of a solution. "If we give this to the wrong people, the foundation will bury it. But if we go to someone with enough power, someone outside their influence, they won't be able to stop it."

"Someone like who?" Jake asked, his voice weary. "We can't exactly walk into a newspaper office with this and expect them to publish it without the foundation shutting it down."

Sarah thought for a moment, then an idea began to take shape. "What about investigative journalists? Someone independent, not tied to the major networks or anyone in the foundation's pocket. There are journalists out there who specialize in exposing corruption, who have the resources to get this out without it being silenced."

"Do you know any?" Alex asked, raising an eyebrow.

Sarah hesitated. "No, but I know someone who might."

Jake turned to her, intrigued. "Who?"

"An old friend of my mom's," Sarah explained. "She was a journalist, and she used to do work on corruption and uncovering hidden organizations. If anyone can get this out to the world, it's her."

"Is she still in the game?" Alex asked. "Because we're running out of time."

"I don't know," Sarah admitted. "But I have her contact info. She's not far from here, about an hour outside of the city. If we can get to her, she might be able to help us."

"That's a risk," Jake said, frowning. "What if she's not who you remember? Or worse, what if she's been compromised?"

Sarah nodded, understanding the fear in his voice. Trust was a luxury they didn't have. But they were running out of options, and they needed someone who could handle the enormity of what they had uncovered.

"It's a risk," Sarah agreed. "But if we don't do something soon, the foundation will catch up to us, and we won't have any options left. We have to take the chance."

Alex glanced in the rearview mirror, checking to make sure they weren't being followed. "Alright, give me the address. We'll go."

Sarah pulled out her phone and found the contact information she hadn't used in years. Her mom had been close friends with this journalist, who had once been a fierce investigative reporter, taking on corporations and political corruption. She hadn't heard from her in a long time, but if she was still working in the field, she might be their only hope.

As they drove, Sarah's mind raced with thoughts of what lay ahead. Would this journalist be willing to help them? Or would she turn them away, too scared of what the foundation might do?

An hour later, they pulled up to a small, secluded house on the outskirts of a quiet town. The lights were on inside, and there was a car parked in the driveway. Sarah's stomach churned with a mixture of hope and fear.

"This is it," she said, her voice barely above a whisper.

"You sure about this?" Jake asked, glancing at the house.

Sarah nodded, though her heart pounded in her chest. "We don't have a choice."

They got out of the car and walked up to the door, the night air cool and still. Sarah hesitated for a moment, then knocked.

After a few moments, the door opened, and a woman in her

fifties stood before them. Her hair was streaked with gray, and there were lines of weariness etched into her face, but her eyes were sharp, curious.

"Can I help you?" she asked, her gaze sweeping over the group with a hint of suspicion.

"Ms. Lawson?" Sarah asked cautiously. "I'm Sarah Keane. My mother, Alice Keane, used to work with you years ago."

Recognition flickered in the woman's eyes, and her posture relaxed slightly. "Alice Keane's daughter? I haven't heard from your mom in years. What are you doing here at this hour?"

Sarah glanced at the others, then back at Ms. Lawson. "I know this is strange, but we need your help. We've uncovered something—something big—and we don't know where else to turn."

Ms. Lawson studied Sarah for a moment, then stepped aside, motioning them inside. "Come in. You'd better tell me everything."

They followed her inside, the warmth of the house a stark contrast to the cold fear Sarah felt inside. They sat around her small kitchen table as Sarah explained everything—the Satori Foundation, the experiments, the missing students, and the evidence they had found. She told Ms. Lawson about Mike's sacrifice and how they were now being hunted by the very organization they were trying to expose.

Ms. Lawson listened intently, her face growing more serious with every word. When Sarah finally pulled out the flash drive, Ms. Lawson's expression hardened.

"This is... bigger than I imagined," Ms. Lawson said quietly, leaning back in her chair. "The Satori Foundation, you say? I've heard whispers about them over the years, but nothing concrete. What you've uncovered could bring them down—but it's dangerous. If they know you have this, they won't stop until they silence you."

"We know," Sarah said softly. "That's why we need your help. We don't know who we can trust, but we can't let them bury this."

Ms. Lawson was silent for a long moment, her eyes narrowing as she stared at the flash drive. Finally, she nodded.

"Alright," she said. "I'm in. I still have contacts—people who can get this out into the world, people the foundation can't easily silence. But we need to move fast. Once they realize what we're doing, they'll come for all of us."

Relief washed over Sarah, though it was tinged with fear. They had taken the first step, but the fight was far from over.

"Thank you," Sarah whispered, her voice thick with emotion.

Ms. Lawson nodded, her expression grim. "Don't thank me yet. This is just the beginning. Now let's get to work."

Ms. Lawson's small kitchen was now a war room. The flash drive was plugged into her old laptop, the screen glowing with a mass of files—photographs, documents, financial records—each one more damning than the last. Sarah and the others sat huddled around the table, the tension in the air thick as Ms. Lawson clicked through the data, her brow furrowed in concentration.

"This is... incredible," Ms. Lawson muttered, her fingers flying over the keyboard as she scanned the files. "I've seen corruption before, but nothing on this scale. The Satori Foundation has its hands in everything—politics, education, even law enforcement. They've built an empire right under everyone's noses."

Sarah nodded, her stomach churning. "We've seen how far their influence reaches. Every time we think we're a step ahead, they're already waiting for us. That's why we need to move fast. We need to get this out before they realize what we've found."

Ms. Lawson glanced at her, her eyes narrowing. "We'll need to be strategic about this. If we leak everything at once, they'll try to discredit it, and they have enough connections to bury the story. But if we expose them piece by piece, we might be able to overwhelm them. We need to hit them where it hurts and leave them scrambling to cover their tracks."

Jake, who had been pacing nervously around the kitchen, stopped and crossed his arms. "How do we do that? We're just a bunch of kids. They have lawyers, politicians, maybe even the media in their pocket."

Ms. Lawson leaned back in her chair, her expression thoughtful. "You're right. They have powerful allies, but so do I. I know a few independent journalists—people who aren't afraid of a fight, people the foundation can't control. I'll get in touch with them, and we'll start planning a series of releases. We'll send out the financial records first—expose their funding sources, show how they've been funneling money into illegal activities. That'll get people's attention."

"And what about the experiments?" Emily asked quietly, her face pale. "What they did to those kids… people need to know about that, too."

Ms. Lawson's expression softened as she nodded. "We'll release that next, but we'll have to time it right. If we drop everything at once, it could get lost in the chaos. We need to keep the pressure on them, keep the story alive until they have no choice but to respond."

Sarah's heart pounded in her chest. It was finally happening. After everything they had been through—after losing Mike, after being hunted by the foundation—they were finally in a position to strike back.

"But there's one problem," Alex said, his voice low. "The foundation isn't just going to sit back and let us expose them. They'll come after us with everything they have. We barely escaped last time, and now that they know we have the evidence..."

"They'll come for us," Sarah finished, her voice grim. "We know. That's why we need to be ready."

Ms. Lawson stood up, her eyes sharp. "You're not wrong. Once they realize we've started releasing this, they'll send their people after you. And they won't stop. But I know how these people operate. They're used to controlling things from behind the scenes, using their money and influence to make problems disappear. If we keep the story in the public eye, they'll have a harder time silencing us."

"And what if they don't care about being subtle anymore?" Jake asked, his voice hard. "What if they decide it's easier to just take us out?"

Ms. Lawson met his gaze, her expression unflinching. "Then we make it as hard as possible for them. I have contacts who can help protect you—people who know how to handle this kind of pressure. But you need to understand something: this isn't just about survival anymore. This is about making sure the truth gets out, no matter what happens to us."

The weight of her words settled over the group like a heavy fog. They had known, deep down, that this was a fight for their lives. But hearing it said so plainly, so bluntly, made it all the more real.

"We're in," Sarah said, her voice steady but determined. "Whatever it takes, we're not stopping until the foundation is exposed."

The others nodded in agreement, though fear flickered in their eyes. They were all afraid—how could they not be?—but they were united in their determination. They couldn't let the Satori Foundation win.

Ms. Lawson walked over to the window, peeking through the blinds. "Alright, then. We have a lot to do and not much time to do it. I'll start contacting the journalists I know. You all need to lay low for the next few days. I have a safe house outside of town—it's not much, but it'll keep you off the grid while we get this story out."

"How long do you think we have before the foundation realizes what's happening?" Emily asked, her voice trembling.

Ms. Lawson turned back to face them, her expression serious. "Not long. A day, maybe two. They're watching everything, but we've got the element of surprise. If we move fast, we can stay ahead of them."

The air in the room felt electric, charged with a mix of fear and anticipation. They were on the brink of something monumental—something that could destroy the Satori Foundation for good. But the danger was closer than ever, and they all knew that if they made even one mistake, it could cost them their lives.

"We should leave tonight," Sarah said, glancing at the others. "The sooner we're off the grid, the better."

Ms. Lawson nodded. "I'll give you the address of the safe house. I'll meet you there once I've made contact with my people."

Sarah gathered her things, her heart pounding as she stuffed the flash drive back into her bag. The tension in the room was suffocating, but there was a renewed sense of purpose in the air. This was it. The countdown had begun, and soon the world would know the truth.

As they prepared to leave, Ms. Lawson pulled Sarah aside, her voice low. "Listen, Sarah. I've been in this game a long time, and I know what people like the Satori Foundation are capable of. But I've also seen what happens when people fight back. You've done something remarkable—something most people wouldn't have the courage to do. But this fight is only going to get harder. You need to be ready for whatever comes next."

Sarah nodded, her throat tight. "I am."

Ms. Lawson squeezed her arm, then stepped back. "Good. Now go. I'll meet you at the safe house in a few hours."

With that, Sarah and the others slipped out into the night, the weight of what they were about to do pressing down on them like a storm cloud. They piled into the car, the air thick with tension as Alex started the engine.

As they drove away from Ms. Lawson's house, Sarah glanced out the window, her heart heavy with both fear and hope. They were about to take on a monster—an enemy that had seemed untouchable just days ago. But now they had a chance. A real chance to bring it all crashing down.

"We're going to win," she whispered, more to herself than anyone else.

The others remained silent, but there was a flicker of determination in their eyes. They knew the risks, but they were ready.

The countdown had begun, and there was no turning back now.

The drive to the safe house felt like it lasted an eternity. The car hummed along the empty back roads, the headlights cutting through the darkness as Alex carefully navigated through the winding paths that led them farther away from the city. It was hard to tell if anyone was following them, but every shadow that moved or flicker of light sent Sarah's heart racing.

The weight of what they were about to do pressed down on her, heavier than ever. They had set something in motion that couldn't be stopped, and the consequences of their actions were hanging over them like a storm ready to break. In her hands, she still clutched the flash drive, the damning evidence that could destroy the Satori Foundation, but it was also a target on their backs.

"How far is this place?" Jake asked from the backseat, his voice low and tense.

"Not much farther," Alex replied, his eyes never leaving the road. "According to the directions Ms. Lawson gave us, it's just a few miles out."

The car went silent again as they continued down the isolated road. Emily, sitting beside Jake, had been quiet ever since they left Ms. Lawson's house. Her face was pale, her hands shaking slightly as she stared out the window.

"Hey," Sarah said softly, turning in her seat to face Emily. "Are you okay?"

Emily blinked, tearing her gaze away from the dark trees outside. She nodded, though her voice trembled when she spoke. "I'm scared, Sarah. We're so close, but it feels like... like everything could go wrong any second."

Sarah reached over, squeezing Emily's hand. "I know. I'm scared too. But we've come this far. We can't back down now."

Emily gave a small nod, her eyes glassy with unshed tears. "It just feels like they're everywhere. Like no matter what we do, they'll find us."

"They won't," Sarah said, trying to sound more confident than she felt. "Ms. Lawson said this place is off the grid. We'll be safe there, at least for a while. Long enough for her to start getting the information out."

"And then what?" Jake asked, leaning forward. "We're just going to wait around while they come after us? Because we both know the foundation isn't going to sit back and let us expose them."

"We'll figure it out," Alex said, though his voice lacked conviction. "One step at a time."

Sarah didn't reply. She couldn't. Deep down, she knew Jake was right. The Satori Foundation wouldn't just sit back while they tore down everything it had built. Once the information was released, they would come for them with everything they had.

They drove in silence for a few more minutes until they finally reached the safe house. It was a small, weathered cabin nestled in the woods, barely visible from the road. The trees crowded around it like silent sentinels, their branches twisting in the wind as though warning them to turn back.

Alex pulled the car into the narrow driveway and turned off the engine. The sudden silence was unnerving, the only sound the faint rustle of leaves in the breeze. They all sat there for a moment, staring at the cabin, none of them moving.

"This is it," Alex said, breaking the silence. "We're here."

They climbed out of the car, the night air cool against their skin. Sarah glanced around, her heart pounding. The place seemed deserted, untouched by anyone for a long time, but that was a good thing. It meant they were far enough off the grid that no one would find them—at least not right away.

The inside of the cabin was just as modest as the outside, with old wooden furniture and a fireplace that hadn't been used in years. It smelled of dust and damp wood, but it was safe, and that was all that mattered.

Alex flicked on the lights, which blinked to life with a faint buzz. "Not bad," he muttered, surveying the small space. "It's not much, but it'll do."

Sarah dropped her bag onto the table, her muscles aching with exhaustion. They had barely slept in days, constantly looking over their shoulders, waiting for the next attack. Now that they were finally somewhere safe, the adrenaline that had been keeping her going started to fade, leaving her drained.

Emily wandered over to the fireplace, staring at the cold hearth. "I don't think I'll ever get used to this," she murmured. "Constantly running, always wondering if this is the last safe place we'll ever see."

"We won't be running forever," Sarah said, though she wasn't sure if she believed her own words. "Once the information is out, once the world knows what the Satori Foundation has done, they won't be able to hide anymore."

"But what about us?" Jake asked, sitting down heavily in one of the old chairs. "What happens when they come after us? Because they will, Sarah. You know they will."

Sarah didn't answer. She didn't have one. All she knew was that they had to finish what they started. They had to expose the truth, no matter the cost.

"We'll figure it out," Alex said again, though he sounded just as uncertain as the rest of them. "For now, we just need to focus on staying safe until Ms. Lawson gets the information out. After that... we'll take it one step at a time."

They spent the next few hours settling in, securing the windows and doors, and making sure the place was as safe as it could be. The sense of relief that came with being off the grid was palpable, but it was laced with an undercurrent of anxiety—like the calm before the storm.

Sarah sat down at the small table in the middle of the cabin, the flash drive still in her hand. She stared at it for a long moment, her thoughts racing. Everything they had risked, everything they had lost, was tied to this tiny piece of technology. Inside it was the evidence that would expose the Satori Foundation's darkest secrets, the proof they needed to take the organization down.

But the more she thought about it, the more a cold dread settled in her stomach. The foundation wouldn't just give up because they had a few documents. They would fight back. And when they did, Sarah wasn't sure they would be able to stand up to them.

She was so lost in thought that she didn't hear Alex approach until he sat down beside her.

"You okay?" he asked quietly, his voice filled with concern.

Sarah nodded, though the truth was, she wasn't sure. "I just… I keep thinking about what happens next. We're so close, but it feels like the closer we get, the more dangerous it becomes."

"It does," Alex agreed, his eyes darkening. "But we knew it wouldn't be easy. The foundation has been controlling everything for years. They're not going to let us take them down without a fight."

Sarah sighed, running a hand through her hair. "I just hope we're ready for it."

Alex placed a hand on her shoulder, giving her a reassuring squeeze. "We'll figure it out, Sarah. We always do."

For a moment, they sat in silence, the weight of everything they had been through pressing down on them. Sarah closed her eyes, the exhaustion catching up with her, but she knew sleep wouldn't come easily.

The countdown had started, and with each passing hour, they were getting closer to the endgame. Soon, the world would know the truth. But with that truth came danger—danger they might not survive.

Sarah tightened her grip on the flash drive, her resolve hardening. They had come too far to turn back now. Whatever happened next, they would face it together.

The Satori Foundation wouldn't win.

Not this time.

The cabin's eerie stillness was only broken by the faint rustling of the wind outside. Sarah lay on a small cot, staring at the wooden beams of the ceiling. Sleep, which she desperately needed, wouldn't come. Every time she closed her eyes, she saw flashes of the past few days—the chase, Mike's sacrifice, Claire's betrayal. And now, as they hid in this forgotten corner of the world, waiting for Ms. Lawson to send word that the first wave of information had gone public, the fear of what was coming next loomed over them like a storm cloud.

She glanced at her phone for the hundredth time. Still nothing from Ms. Lawson.

"Are you okay?" Emily's voice came from across the room, barely a whisper.

Sarah turned to see Emily sitting up in bed, her eyes wide and worried. "Yeah," Sarah lied. "Just thinking."

"I can't stop thinking either," Emily admitted. "What if Ms. Lawson doesn't get the information out in time? What if—"

"She will," Sarah interrupted gently. "She knows how to do this. She's done it before."

Emily didn't look convinced, and truthfully, neither was Sarah. But there was no point in spiraling into fear. Not yet.

Sarah swung her legs off the cot and stood up, stretching

her stiff muscles. She crossed the small room and stood by the window, peering out into the dark forest. The trees swayed gently in the breeze, their silhouettes like dark sentinels guarding the cabin. Somewhere out there, she knew, the Satori Foundation's men were searching for them. It was only a matter of time before they found them.

She heard movement behind her as Alex entered the room. "Still nothing?" he asked, his voice low.

"Nothing," Sarah replied, frustration creeping into her voice. "I hate this waiting. It feels like we're just sitting ducks, waiting for them to strike."

"We won't be waiting forever," Alex said, his tone reassuring. "Ms. Lawson knows what she's doing. Once the first wave of information is out, the foundation will be too busy trying to control the fallout to come after us."

"Yeah, but what if they find us before that happens?" Jake's voice came from the doorway. He had been standing just outside, listening. "We're counting on them not finding us here, but what if they already have?"

Sarah frowned. "They haven't found us yet, Jake. We're safe for now."

"But for how long?" Jake pressed. "Think about it—this is the Satori Foundation we're dealing with. They have resources, connections. They're relentless. What makes you think they won't track us down, even here?"

Sarah didn't have an answer. She hated that Jake was right, but the truth was, no place felt safe anymore. The foundation had been one step ahead of them for so long, and now, they were playing a dangerous game of cat and mouse.

Before anyone could respond, Sarah's phone buzzed in her hand, startling her. Her heart raced as she saw Ms. Lawson's name flash across the screen. Without hesitation, she answered.

"Ms. Lawson?" she said, her voice tight with anticipation.

"Sarah," Ms. Lawson's voice crackled through the speaker, and the tension in her tone made Sarah's stomach drop. "We've got a problem."

Sarah's heart sank. "What kind of problem?"

"The foundation knows. Somehow, they've caught wind that we're about to go public. They've mobilized their forces, and they're moving fast. I'm safe for now, but I don't know for how long. And, Sarah... I think they know where you are."

Sarah's blood ran cold. "What do you mean?"

"I've been monitoring their communications," Ms. Lawson explained, her voice urgent. "They've been tracking your movements since the Nexus. They're getting close. I don't know how they found you, but you need to get out of there—now."

Sarah's heart raced as she turned to the others. "We need to leave," she said, her voice barely steady. "They know where we are."

Alex's eyes widened. "Are you serious?"

Sarah nodded, her mind racing. "Ms. Lawson says they've tracked us. We don't have much time."

"How?" Jake asked, his voice thick with panic. "We've been careful! How could they know?"

"It doesn't matter how," Sarah said, her voice firm. "What matters is that we need to go. Now."

They scrambled into action, grabbing their bags and anything else they could carry. The safe house, which had felt like their sanctuary just hours ago, now felt like a trap—a ticking time bomb about to go off. Sarah's pulse raced as she tried to focus on the next step. Where would they go? How would they stay ahead of the foundation now?

As they rushed outside to the car, Sarah's phone buzzed again. She glanced down and saw a message from Ms. Lawson: *Keep moving. I'll contact you when it's safe. Don't stop.*

Alex started the engine, and the car roared to life, but before he could pull out of the driveway, headlights appeared at the end of the narrow road.

"Is that them?" Emily asked, her voice trembling.

"Go!" Sarah shouted, her heart slamming in her chest. "Drive!"

Alex floored the gas pedal, and the car lurched forward, speeding down the narrow dirt road. The headlights behind them followed, growing closer with every second.

"They've found us," Jake muttered, his voice filled with dread.

The car raced down the winding road, the trees flashing by in a blur as the foundation's men gained on them. Sarah gripped the seat, her mind spinning as the weight of the situation pressed down on her. They couldn't outrun them forever. They needed a plan.

"Turn off here!" Sarah shouted, pointing to a narrow side road that branched off from the main path.

Alex swerved onto the road, the tires skidding on the loose dirt. For a moment, it felt like they might have lost their pursuers, but then the headlights reappeared, this time closer than before.

"They're still on us!" Jake shouted.

Panic surged through Sarah as she frantically tried to think of a way out. The road ahead was a dead end. They were trapped.

"Alex, stop the car," Sarah said suddenly, her voice calm despite the terror racing through her veins.

"What?" Alex asked, glancing at her in disbelief.

"Stop the car," she repeated, her voice firm. "We need to make a stand."

Alex hesitated for a moment, but then he slammed on the brakes, bringing the car to a screeching halt. The foundation's car skidded to a stop behind them, and Sarah could see the figures inside moving, preparing to confront them.

"This is crazy," Jake muttered, his voice shaking.

"We don't have another choice," Sarah said, her hands trembling as she reached for the door handle. "We can't keep running. We end this now."

The others looked at her, fear etched on their faces, but they nodded. One by one, they stepped out of the car, standing together as the foundation's men approached.

As the car doors opened and the men stepped out, Sarah's heart pounded in her chest. There were three of them, all wearing dark suits, their expressions cold and calculating.

"This is the end of the road," one of the men said, his voice low and menacing. "You've run long enough."

Sarah squared her shoulders, her pulse racing. "We have the truth. And the world's going to see it."

The man smirked. "We'll see about that."

Before anyone could move, a gunshot rang out, splitting the night air.

The sound of the gunshot echoed through the still night, and for a heartbeat, everything stopped. Sarah froze, her breath caught in her throat, as the world seemed to hold its breath with her. She didn't know who had fired the shot, but in that split second, she feared the worst.

Then, chaos erupted.

Jake grabbed Sarah's arm, pulling her behind the car for cover. Emily and Alex followed, crouching down as the men from the Satori Foundation scrambled, clearly not expecting the resistance. Another shot rang out, and Sarah instinctively ducked, her heart pounding in her ears.

"They're not playing around," Alex muttered, glancing over the car's hood to get a look at their attackers.

"No kidding!" Jake hissed, his face pale as he looked at Sarah. "What do we do? We're pinned down!"

Sarah's mind raced. They couldn't just sit here and wait for the inevitable. The foundation's men were closing in, and they were armed. If they didn't act fast, they wouldn't survive this.

"Split up," Sarah said, her voice shaky but determined. "If we spread out, we'll be harder to hit. Alex, you take Emily and head into the trees. Jake and I will create a diversion."

"Are you crazy?" Jake snapped. "You want us to make ourselves more of a target?"

"It's the only chance we have," Sarah insisted. "They can't take all of us if we're not in the same place. We'll draw their fire, and you two can circle around. Maybe we can take them by surprise."

Alex nodded, though his face was tight with fear. "She's right. It's risky, but it's the only shot we've got."

Emily's eyes were wide with terror, but she nodded too, clinging to Alex as they prepared to run.

"On my signal," Sarah whispered, her heart thudding in her chest. "Go!"

Sarah darted out from behind the car, Jake right on her heels. She could hear the foundation's men shouting, their footsteps pounding the ground as they chased after them. Adrenaline surged through Sarah's veins, fueling her legs as she sprinted toward the dense line of trees.

Another gunshot cracked through the night, missing them

by inches. Sarah felt the sting of a tree branch slashing across her arm, but she didn't stop. She and Jake darted into the cover of the trees, weaving through the trunks as fast as they could.

Behind them, the foundation's men were following, but Sarah had no intention of letting them catch her. She grabbed a fallen branch as she ran, hoping they could buy enough time for Alex and Emily to get into position.

"We're not going to outrun them forever," Jake panted, his voice laced with panic. "They're getting closer!"

Sarah knew he was right. They had moments, maybe seconds, before the foundation's men caught up with them. Her lungs burned, her muscles screamed for rest, but she pushed through it, searching for anything that could give them an edge.

"Over here!" Sarah shouted, hoping to lure the men farther into the woods. If Alex and Emily could get behind them, they might have a chance to turn the tables.

But just as Sarah turned to glance over her shoulder, she stumbled on a root, falling hard to the ground. Pain shot through her leg, but she bit back a cry, scrambling to her feet.

"Sarah!" Jake yelled, reaching for her. But it was too late.

One of the foundation's men burst through the trees, his gun raised and aimed directly at Sarah. Her heart stopped. She had nowhere to run, nowhere to hide. This was it.

"Don't move," the man growled, his voice cold and merciless.

Sarah's mind raced. She could feel her pulse pounding in her throat, the weight of the flash drive still in her pocket. Everything they had worked for—everything they had lost—was hanging by a thread. And in that moment, she realized that this was more than just a fight for survival. It was a fight for the truth, for justice. And she wasn't about to give up.

"Get down!" a voice yelled from behind the man.

It was Alex.

Before the man could react, Alex tackled him from the side, sending them both crashing to the ground. The gun flew out of the man's hand, skidding across the forest floor. Sarah scrambled to her feet as Jake grabbed the gun, holding it up, though his hands shook violently.

"Don't move!" Jake warned the man, though his voice cracked with fear.

The man glared up at them from the ground, fury etched on his face, but he didn't move.

"Where's the other one?" Sarah asked, glancing around frantically. There had been three men, but only one was here.

Alex breathed heavily, his face pale from the fight. "I don't know. Emily's still back there, but—"

Before he could finish, a gunshot rang out from deeper in the woods. Sarah's blood ran cold.

"Emily," she whispered.

Without thinking, she bolted toward the sound, her heart in her throat. The others followed, their footsteps pounding behind her, but Sarah's mind was focused on one thing—finding Emily.

They raced through the trees, the darkness pressing in on them, until finally, they saw her.

Emily stood in a small clearing, trembling, her hands clutching a gun that was still smoking. At her feet lay the third man from the foundation, motionless.

Sarah stopped, her breath catching in her throat as she took in the scene. Emily's face was pale, her eyes wide with shock.

"I… I didn't mean to…" Emily stammered, her voice barely a whisper. "He… he was going to…"

Sarah rushed to her side, pulling her into a tight embrace.

"It's okay," she whispered. "You did what you had to."

Emily's body shook with silent sobs, and Sarah held her, feeling the weight of everything that had just happened crash down on her. They had survived, but at a cost none of them had anticipated.

The others joined them in the clearing, their faces grim. Alex glanced down at the man on the ground, then back at Sarah.

"What now?" he asked quietly.

Sarah released Emily and straightened, her heart still racing, but her mind clear. "We keep moving. The foundation's not going to stop coming after us, but we have the proof. We need to get it out, no matter what."

"But where do we go?" Jake asked, his voice shaky. "They'll be looking for us everywhere now."

"We go back to Ms. Lawson," Sarah said, her voice firm. "She'll know what to do next. We're not done yet."

They stood there for a moment longer, the weight of everything settling over them. They had won a small battle tonight, but the war was far from over. The Satori Foundation was still out there, still powerful, and they wouldn't stop until they had silenced them for good.

But Sarah wasn't afraid anymore. They had come too far to turn back now. The truth was within reach, and she wasn't going to let it slip away.

"Let's go," Sarah said, her voice steady.

And together, they disappeared into the night, determined to see this through to the very end.

The Reckoning

The safe house felt miles away as the group drove in tense silence, the events of the last few hours weighing heavily on their minds. The night had become a blur of gunfire, close calls, and adrenaline-fueled decisions, but now, as the dark road stretched before them, there was no denying that they were getting closer to the end of the line. The weight of their mission—exposing the Satori Foundation—felt heavier than ever.

Sarah sat in the passenger seat, her eyes fixed on the road ahead, though her mind was far away. Emily was slumped in the backseat, staring blankly out the window, still processing what had happened in the woods. She had saved their lives by pulling the trigger, but the toll it had taken on her was written all over her face.

"How are you holding up?" Alex asked quietly from behind the wheel, glancing over at Sarah.

"I'm fine," Sarah lied, her voice tight. In reality, she felt like she was balancing on the edge of a cliff. The fear, the guilt, the exhaustion—they were all threatening to pull her under. But she couldn't afford to fall apart. Not now. Not when they were so close.

Alex didn't push. He just nodded and kept his eyes on the

road.

The small safe house they had fled from earlier now felt like their only refuge. Ms. Lawson had promised to meet them there once she had secured a way to release the information, but Sarah couldn't shake the fear gnawing at her that the foundation was closing in faster than they could react.

"What if she doesn't make it?" Jake asked from the backseat, his voice thick with worry. "What if something happens to her before she can release the files?"

"She'll make it," Sarah said, though the knot in her stomach told her otherwise. "Ms. Lawson is smart. She's been playing this game a long time. She'll know how to stay ahead of them."

Jake didn't respond, but the tension in the car was palpable. None of them wanted to voice their deepest fear—that the foundation was always one step ahead. They had fought and survived longer than they had expected, but the enemy was relentless. They had seen firsthand how far the foundation was willing to go to protect its secrets.

Finally, after what felt like hours, the safe house came into view. It was small and unremarkable, nestled among a dense line of trees. Alex pulled the car up the narrow driveway and killed the engine, leaving them in the deafening silence of the night.

Sarah's pulse quickened as they climbed out of the car, scanning the dark surroundings for any sign of movement. The cabin seemed untouched, just as they had left it. But that didn't mean they were safe.

"Do you think they followed us?" Emily asked, her voice barely above a whisper.

"I don't think so," Alex replied, but there was an edge of uncertainty in his voice.

They made their way inside, the cabin's familiar walls offering a brief moment of respite. But Sarah couldn't shake the gnawing feeling of unease in her gut. Every second they stayed here felt like a gamble, and with the foundation closing in, time was running out.

The flash drive felt heavy in Sarah's pocket, its presence a constant reminder of the stakes. Everything they had risked, everything they had lost, was tied to this tiny piece of technology. Inside it were the files that would expose the Satori Foundation—the key to taking down the very organization that had hunted them from the shadows.

But that key also made them targets.

"We should check the perimeter," Jake said, his voice laced with tension. "Make sure we're alone."

Alex nodded. "Good idea. I'll go with you."

Sarah watched as they stepped outside, leaving her and Emily alone in the small living room. The air felt thick with the unspoken dread that had settled over them. They were so close, but the danger was pressing down on them from all sides.

"You okay?" Sarah asked, turning to Emily, who was still staring at the floor, her hands trembling slightly.

Emily shook her head. "No," she whispered. "I don't know if I'll ever be okay again."

Sarah's heart ached for her friend. She wanted to say something comforting, something that would make it all better, but there were no words that could undo the trauma they had endured. Instead, she sat down beside her, placing a hand on Emily's shoulder.

"You saved our lives," Sarah said softly. "What you did out there—it wasn't easy, but you did it because you had to. And I'm so grateful for that."

Emily didn't respond, but a tear slipped down her cheek. Sarah pulled her into a gentle hug, wishing she could take some of the pain away.

Before she could say anything more, the door swung open, and Alex and Jake rushed back inside, their faces pale.

"We've got a problem," Jake said, his voice tight with urgency.

Sarah's heart skipped a beat. "What is it?"

"They're here," Alex said, his voice low. "There's a car parked a few hundred yards down the road. It's them, Sarah. The foundation's men."

Panic surged through Sarah's chest, but she forced herself to stay calm. "How many?"

"At least two, maybe three," Alex replied. "We saw them getting out of the car, but they haven't made their move yet. They don't know we've spotted them."

Sarah's mind raced. This was it. They were cornered. The foundation had found them, and there was nowhere left to run.

"What do we do?" Emily asked, her voice shaking.

"We fight," Sarah said, her voice steely with determination. "We're not letting them take us—not after everything we've been through."

"But we're outnumbered," Jake said, fear creeping into his voice. "How are we supposed to fight them?"

"We don't have to beat them," Sarah replied, her mind working fast. "We just have to hold them off long enough for Ms. Lawson to release the information. Once it's out, they lose their leverage."

"But how long do we have?" Alex asked.

Sarah pulled out her phone, her hands trembling slightly as she sent a message to Ms. Lawson. *They found us. How close are we?*

A few seconds later, her phone buzzed with a reply. *Almost there. Stay hidden. Just a little longer.*

"We just need to hold them off for a few more minutes," Sarah said, glancing at the others. "If we can keep them from getting to us until Ms. Lawson releases the files, we'll have won."

The weight of her words hung in the air as the group exchanged glances. They had fought so hard to get to this point, but now they were staring down their final battle. If they could just survive a little longer, the Satori Foundation's secrets would be exposed for the world to see.

"Okay," Jake said, steeling himself. "Let's do this."

They quickly barricaded the doors and windows, preparing for the inevitable confrontation. Every creak, every rustle of leaves outside felt like a countdown to the moment the foundation's men would make their move.

Sarah stood by the window, her pulse racing as she clutched the flash drive in her hand. She knew this was it. This was the moment that would determine everything—whether they lived or died, whether the foundation was brought down or continued its reign of terror.

As the minutes ticked by, Sarah felt a strange calm settle over her. They were outnumbered, outgunned, and cornered, but they weren't beaten. Not yet.

And they were ready to fight for the truth.

The air inside the cabin was thick with tension. Every second felt like an eternity as Sarah and the others braced themselves for the inevitable confrontation. Outside, the foundation's men were lurking in the shadows, waiting to strike. The distant crunch of footsteps on gravel echoed through the trees, growing louder, closer.

Alex moved to the window, his body tense as he scanned

the darkened landscape. "They're moving toward the cabin," he whispered, his voice low but urgent. "They'll be on us any minute."

Sarah's heart pounded in her chest, her mind racing. They had prepared as best they could—barricaded the windows, blocked the doors—but deep down, she knew it wouldn't be enough. The foundation's men were professionals, armed and trained, and they wouldn't hesitate to break through whatever defenses the group had hastily thrown together.

"We stick to the plan," Sarah said, trying to keep her voice steady. "We hold them off as long as we can. Ms. Lawson is close to releasing the files. We just need to buy a little more time."

Jake's face was pale, but he nodded, gripping the small knife they had found in the kitchen. "What if they get in?" he asked, his voice trembling slightly.

"Then we make sure they don't get to the flash drive," Sarah replied, holding it up for emphasis. "Whatever happens, we can't let them take this."

Emily, who had been sitting in silence, stood up slowly, her face a mask of determination. "We've come too far to lose now," she said quietly. "We can't let them win."

Sarah felt a surge of pride at Emily's resolve, but the fear still gnawed at her. They were outnumbered, and every instinct screamed that this was a losing battle. But they had no choice. The truth was in their hands, and if they fell now, it would be buried forever.

The sound of the footsteps stopped just outside the door. For a moment, there was only silence, the kind that weighed heavy and oppressive, like the calm before a storm. Sarah tightened her grip on the flash drive, her breath coming in shallow bursts.

Then, without warning, the door rattled violently as someone tried to force it open.

"They're here," Alex hissed, backing away from the window.

The door shook again, harder this time, the force of the impact sending splinters of wood flying into the room. Sarah's pulse spiked as she glanced at the others. There was no time left.

"Take positions!" she ordered, her voice low but firm.

Alex and Jake moved to either side of the door, while Sarah and Emily crouched near the back of the room, ready to defend the flash drive at all costs. The air was thick with tension as they waited, the pounding of the door growing more intense with every hit.

Finally, with a deafening crack, the door gave way.

The men from the foundation stormed in, their faces hard, guns raised, moving with the precision of people who had done this many times before. Sarah's heart lurched in her chest, but there was no time to be afraid.

Alex was the first to move, swinging a heavy wooden plank at the nearest man. The blow landed with a sickening thud, and the man stumbled back, but he didn't go down. Jake lunged at another, his knife flashing in the dim light, but the man sidestepped easily, slamming Jake into the wall.

"Get back!" one of the men shouted, his gun trained on Sarah.

Sarah's mind raced. They were outnumbered, outmatched. She had to do something. She had to protect the flash drive. Without thinking, she darted toward the back door, the small, rarely used exit that led out into the woods behind the cabin.

"Go!" she shouted to Emily. "Get out of here! Take the drive!"

Emily hesitated for only a second before grabbing the flash drive from Sarah's hand and bolting for the door. Sarah followed, her heart pounding in her ears as the foundation's men shouted behind them. They burst out into the cool night air, the darkness of the woods closing in around them.

"Run!" Sarah urged, her breath ragged as she and Emily sprinted into the forest.

The sound of gunshots rang out behind them, and Sarah's blood ran cold. She didn't know if the others were still holding the line or if they had fallen, but right now, all that mattered was getting the flash drive to safety. The truth had to come out, no matter the cost.

The trees blurred as they ran, branches whipping at their faces, the uneven ground threatening to trip them with every step. Sarah's lungs burned, and her legs ached, but she didn't stop. She couldn't stop.

Behind them, she could hear the shouts of the foundation's men, their footsteps crashing through the underbrush. They were gaining on them.

"We can't outrun them," Emily panted, her face pale with fear.

Sarah's mind raced. She knew Emily was right. They couldn't keep running forever. The foundation's men were too close, too fast. They needed a new plan.

"Hide!" Sarah hissed, grabbing Emily's arm and pulling her behind a thick tree. They crouched low, holding their breath as the sound of footsteps grew louder, closer.

Sarah's heart pounded in her chest, every muscle in her body screaming with tension. If the men found them now, it was over. They had no weapons, no way to fight back. But if they could just stay hidden long enough for the men to pass, they might have a chance.

The footsteps slowed, and for a moment, Sarah thought they had been spotted. She could see the faint outline of one of the men, his gun raised as he scanned the trees. Her breath caught in her throat, and she pressed herself harder against the bark, willing herself to be invisible.

Then, after what felt like an eternity, the man moved on, disappearing into the darkness.

Sarah exhaled slowly, her hands shaking as she glanced at Emily. "We need to keep moving," she whispered.

Emily nodded, her eyes wide with fear but her resolve unbroken. They stood up slowly, moving as quietly as they could through the trees, putting as much distance as possible between themselves and the foundation's men.

As they moved deeper into the forest, the sound of footsteps faded, replaced by the distant hum of night insects and the soft rustle of leaves. For the first time since they had left the cabin, Sarah allowed herself to believe they might actually make it out of this alive.

"We're almost there," Sarah whispered. "Just a little longer."

But just as she said the words, the crack of a gunshot echoed through the trees.

Sarah felt a sharp pain in her side, and the world seemed to tilt around her. She stumbled, her vision blurring as she tried to stay on her feet.

"Sarah!" Emily cried, rushing to her side.

Sarah clutched her side, her hand coming away wet with blood. She tried to speak, to tell Emily to keep running, but her voice wouldn't come.

"No," Emily whispered, her face pale with shock. "No, no, no..."

Sarah's knees buckled, and she collapsed to the ground, the pain radiating through her body like fire. She could hear Emily's panicked voice, but it was distant, muffled, as if it were coming from underwater.

All she could think about was the flash drive—the truth that was still out there, waiting to be revealed.

"Go," Sarah whispered, her voice barely audible. "You have to..."

But her vision was already fading, the darkness closing in.

And as the world slipped away, she could only hope that Emily would make it.

That the truth would finally come out.

The world around Sarah faded in and out as pain shot through her side, her consciousness clinging to the fragile thread that kept her present. She felt Emily's hands gripping her shoulders, trying to shake her awake, but her body refused to respond. The cold forest floor pressed against her cheek, and everything seemed to blur, the edges of her vision darkening.

"Sarah, please, hold on!" Emily's voice was frantic, thick with panic. "Don't leave me. We're so close!"

Sarah struggled to focus, to stay conscious, but the pain was overwhelming. She could feel the blood soaking through her shirt, warm and sticky against her skin. Each shallow breath sent a fresh wave of agony through her body. She knew she didn't have much time. The Satori Foundation's men were still out there, and the chance of survival was slipping through her fingers like sand.

The flash drive. That was all that mattered now. The truth had to get out.

Sarah forced herself to focus, her vision swimming as she reached out and grabbed Emily's arm. "Take it," she whispered, her voice hoarse and barely audible.

Emily looked down, tears streaking her face, her expression one of utter terror. "No, I'm not leaving you. I can't!"

"You have to," Sarah rasped, her grip tightening on Emily's wrist. "Get the drive to Ms. Lawson. She'll know what to do. This… this is bigger than us."

Emily shook her head, her tears falling freely now. "I can't do this without you, Sarah."

"You have to," Sarah repeated, forcing the words out despite the searing pain in her side. "The world needs to know. If we don't stop the foundation… they'll keep hurting people. They'll keep controlling everything."

Emily's hands trembled as she clutched the flash drive to her chest, her eyes filled with fear and anguish. She hesitated, torn between staying with Sarah and running to finish what they had started.

"I'll come back for you," Emily whispered, her voice breaking. "I promise."

Sarah wanted to believe her, wanted to cling to the hope that Emily could make it back in time. But deep down, she knew that wasn't how this was going to play out. She had made her peace with that.

"You have to go, now," Sarah urged, her voice fading as her strength drained away. "Before they catch up."

Emily bit her lip, nodding through her tears. "I'll get it out, Sarah. I'll make sure everyone knows."

With one last, desperate look at Sarah, Emily stood up, clutching the flash drive tightly in her hand. Sarah watched through blurry eyes as her friend turned and ran into the darkness of the forest, her footsteps quickly swallowed by the shadows.

And then, Sarah was alone.

The pain in her side was getting worse, the blood loss making her head spin. The night was eerily silent now, the danger of the foundation's men pressing down on her like a weight she couldn't shake. Her breath came in shallow gasps, each one a struggle.

She wanted to believe Emily would make it—that she would get the files to Ms. Lawson, expose the foundation, and end this nightmare. But doubt gnawed at her, and the reality of her situation hit her like a punch to the gut. She might not survive this.

But if Emily could escape, if she could get the flash drive out, maybe it would all be worth it.

Hold on, Sarah told herself, but it was getting harder to focus. The pain was consuming her, and her vision was growing darker by the second. The forest around her seemed to close in, and a deep, bone-chilling cold settled over her.

Suddenly, the sound of footsteps echoed through the trees again, louder this time. Sarah's heart lurched. She didn't know if it was Emily coming back, or the foundation's men finally catching up with her. But she was too weak to move, too weak to even call out.

The footsteps grew closer, and Sarah's heart pounded in her chest. She tried to push herself up, but her arms felt like lead, too heavy to lift. Her entire body was shutting down, and she knew, in that moment, she was at the mercy of whoever found her.

Then, out of the corner of her eye, Sarah saw a figure emerge from the trees.

It wasn't Emily.

A man stepped into the clearing, his face obscured by the shadows, but there was no mistaking the cold, calculating demeanor of one of the foundation's agents. His eyes scanned the area before they landed on Sarah's crumpled form, a satisfied smirk crossing his face.

"So," he said quietly, his voice carrying the weight of inevitability, "this is where it ends."

Sarah's heart raced, but she couldn't move. Her limbs were numb, her vision fading, and all she could do was stare up at the man as he approached. The smirk on his face told her everything she needed to know—he didn't see her as a threat anymore. He thought he had won.

But even as the cold fear gripped her, a small spark of defiance flared in Sarah's chest. The foundation hadn't won. Not yet.

She forced herself to speak, though her voice was barely a whisper. "You… won't stop us."

The man crouched down beside her, his expression unreadable. "You're brave. I'll give you that. But bravery doesn't change anything. The Satori Foundation has been in control for a long time. People like you—idealists—always think they can change things. But you're just one person. You're insignificant."

Sarah's vision blurred, but she didn't look away. She wouldn't give him the satisfaction.

"You… don't get it," she whispered, her voice weaker now. "It's not… just me."

The man's smile faltered slightly, and for a moment, he seemed to hesitate.

"The truth is already out there," Sarah continued, her words barely more than a breath. "You can't stop it."

The man stood up slowly, his expression darkening. "We'll see about that."

Sarah's eyes fluttered shut as exhaustion finally overtook her. The last thing she saw before darkness claimed her was the man turning away, disappearing into the shadows once again.

But even as the world slipped away, Sarah held onto that

flicker of hope—that Emily would get the drive out, that Ms. Lawson would expose the Satori Foundation, that the truth would come to light.

Because in the end, the truth was the only thing that mattered.

And it was bigger than all of them.

Emily ran harder than she ever had in her life, the weight of the flash drive heavy in her pocket, and the crushing reality of what had just happened gnawing at her. The cold night air burned her lungs, her legs ached, but she didn't stop. She couldn't stop. Sarah's blood was on her hands, her friend's voice echoing in her mind: *You have to go, now.*

Tears streamed down her face, but she refused to let herself break. Sarah had given her this one task—*Get the drive to Ms. Lawson. Make sure the world knows the truth.* That was all that mattered now. She owed Sarah that much.

The forest was a blur around her as she sprinted through the darkness, every shadow a reminder that the foundation's men were still out there, hunting her. Every sound seemed amplified—the crunch of leaves underfoot, the snap of branches. She felt exposed, vulnerable, but she forced herself to push those thoughts aside.

You can do this, she told herself. *You have to.*

Emily had no idea how far she had run when the dim glow of lights appeared in the distance. Her heart leaped in her chest. It was Ms. Lawson's rendezvous point—the place they had agreed to meet if anything went wrong.

Hope flared in her chest, but it was quickly tempered by fear. What if the foundation had gotten to Ms. Lawson first? What if this was another trap? But Emily had no other option. She had to believe in Ms. Lawson.

As she reached the edge of the clearing, her eyes darted

around, scanning the area for any sign of movement. There were no men in suits, no cars lurking in the shadows. Just the quiet, still night.

She took a deep breath, then stepped forward.

"Emily!"

The sound of Ms. Lawson's voice was a shock to her system. She turned to see the older woman standing beside a dark SUV, her expression one of pure relief.

"Ms. Lawson," Emily gasped, stumbling toward her, her legs barely able to hold her up anymore.

"You made it," Ms. Lawson said, rushing forward and catching Emily as she collapsed into her arms. "Thank God. Are you hurt?"

"No," Emily panted, her hands shaking as she pulled the flash drive from her pocket. "But... Sarah... they shot her. She's still out there."

Ms. Lawson's face tightened, her eyes dark with sorrow. "I'm so sorry, Emily. I know you've been through hell, but you did it. You got the drive."

Emily nodded, her throat tight with emotion as she pressed the flash drive into Ms. Lawson's hand. "This has everything. The experiments, the missing kids, the financial records—it's all on there."

Ms. Lawson's eyes flashed with grim determination. "I'll get it out, Emily. I've already contacted my people. The journalists I trust are standing by, waiting for the files. Once this hits, there's no going back for the foundation. They'll be finished."

Emily sank to the ground, her body trembling with exhaustion, but a flicker of hope bloomed in her chest. "It's over, then. The foundation is done."

Ms. Lawson knelt beside her, her face serious. "It's not over yet. We've exposed the truth, but the foundation is powerful. They'll try to cover this up, discredit the evidence. But this time, they won't be able to stop it. We've got too many eyes on this now."

Emily nodded, wiping at her tears. She felt an overwhelming sense of relief, but it was laced with a deep sadness. Sarah wasn't here to see it. Mike wasn't here. So many had been lost along the way, but at least their sacrifices wouldn't be in vain.

Ms. Lawson stood up, motioning toward the SUV. "Come on. We need to get you somewhere safe. Once this goes public, the foundation will come after everyone connected to this. You need to lie low until the dust settles."

Emily hesitated, her heart heavy. "And Sarah? What about her? We can't just leave her out there."

Ms. Lawson's expression softened. "We'll send someone for her. Right now, you've done what you needed to do. It's time to make sure you're safe."

Emily didn't want to leave, didn't want to abandon Sarah, but deep down, she knew Ms. Lawson was right. She had completed her mission. The truth was in the right hands now, and the world would finally know the horrors the Satori Foundation had been hiding.

As they climbed into the SUV, Emily's hands were still shaking, but for the first time in days, there was a glimmer of hope. They had done it. The foundation was going to fall.

Ms. Lawson started the engine, and they drove off into the night, leaving the dark forest behind. The tension in the air was palpable, but there was a sense of finality now—a sense that the nightmare was almost over.

Emily leaned her head against the window, staring out at the passing trees, her thoughts drifting back to Sarah, to the moments they had fought side by side, to the sacrifices they had made. Sarah had been the bravest person she had ever known, and now she was gone.

Tears welled up in Emily's eyes again, but she blinked them back. She couldn't break now. Not when they were so close to victory.

Suddenly, Ms. Lawson's phone buzzed. She glanced at the screen, her eyes narrowing.

"It's started," she said, her voice tight with anticipation. "The first wave of files has gone live. The journalists are publishing the financial records. People are already talking. By tomorrow morning, the foundation's name will be all over the news."

Emily's heart leapt. *It's happening.*

"They're trying to spin it already," Ms. Lawson continued, her eyes scanning the updates on her phone. "But it's not working. There's too much evidence. The world is finally seeing them for what they are."

Emily felt a rush of vindication, but it was bittersweet. The foundation was being exposed, but the cost had been so high. She thought of Sarah, of Mike, and of the countless lives that had been destroyed by the foundation's greed and cruelty.

But now, at least, there was justice. The world would know.

As they drove into the night, the weight of everything they had endured began to lift, replaced by a quiet resolve. They had won, but the fight wasn't over yet.

The Satori Foundation was crumbling, but Emily knew there were still battles to come. There would be backlash, and the foundation's remnants would try to strike back. But for now, in this moment, they had won a decisive victory.

And that was enough.

As the SUV sped down the road, Emily closed her eyes, letting herself rest for the first time in what felt like forever.

The truth had finally been unleashed.

The first rays of dawn were breaking over the horizon as the SUV pulled into a secluded safe house far outside the city. The drive had been long, but Ms. Lawson hadn't taken any chances. They had switched vehicles twice, taken backroads, and kept their phones off the entire journey. Emily sat in the passenger seat, her body numb from exhaustion, her mind reeling from the events of the night.

The news had already started to spread like wildfire. The Satori Foundation's name was trending across every major media outlet, the story breaking in real-time as the files were leaked. It was happening—the fall of the foundation was in motion.

Emily watched from the window as Ms. Lawson parked the car and cut the engine. The small cabin in front of them looked quiet, unassuming, but there was a sense of safety about it. For the first time in days, Emily felt like she could breathe.

"You did it," Ms. Lawson said softly, turning to Emily. "You and Sarah. You made sure the world knows the truth."

Emily swallowed hard, her throat tight. The victory felt hollow without Sarah beside her. "It was Sarah," Emily whispered, her voice breaking. "She gave everything to make sure this happened."

Ms. Lawson reached out and gently touched Emily's shoulder. "She would be proud of you, Emily. You kept going when it would've been easier to stop. You made sure her sacrifice wasn't for nothing."

Emily nodded, but the grief was still raw. She had won the fight, but it had cost her one of her best friends. It had cost so much more than she had imagined when this all started.

"We'll stay here for a while," Ms. Lawson said, glancing around the quiet surroundings. "The foundation's remnants will be scrambling, but we've dealt them a blow they won't recover from. I have some friends in law enforcement keeping an eye on things. We're safe here."

Emily opened the door and stepped out into the cool morning air. The sun was just beginning to rise, casting a golden light over the trees. Birds chirped in the distance, and for a brief moment, the world seemed peaceful—like it hadn't just been torn apart by secrets and betrayal.

She walked a few steps away from the car, breathing deeply, trying to let the reality of it all sink in. The Satori Foundation was being dismantled. The world knew about the missing students, the illegal experiments, the corruption that had been hidden for so long. There was no going back now.

But there was still a gaping hole in her heart where Sarah's presence should have been. Emily couldn't stop thinking about her, about how brave she had been to the very end. The guilt weighed heavily on her—guilt that she had run while Sarah had stayed behind, guilt that she had survived while her friend had fallen.

"Emily," Ms. Lawson called softly, walking up beside her. "I know this is hard. I know you're carrying a lot of pain right now, but you need to remember something: you didn't run because you were scared. You ran because Sarah asked you to. She trusted you to finish this."

Emily blinked back the tears that had been threatening to fall. "I just… I wish she were here to see it. I wish Mike were here too."

Ms. Lawson nodded, her expression somber. "They're not here, but their fight is still alive in you. They gave their lives for something bigger than themselves. And because of that, countless others will be saved. The truth is out now. The foundation's power is broken."

Emily let Ms. Lawson's words sink in, but the grief was still there, sharp and biting. She knew it would take time to heal—time to come to terms with everything they had lost. But there was a small sense of peace in knowing they had done what they set out to do. The Satori Foundation had been exposed, and their control was crumbling.

"I'm going to make sure the world never forgets what they did," Emily said, her voice quiet but firm. "I'm going to make sure people remember Sarah, and Mike, and everyone else who suffered because of them."

Ms. Lawson smiled softly. "I think you will, Emily. I think you're going to do great things."

They stood there for a few moments in silence, watching as the sun rose higher into the sky, casting warm light over the landscape. It felt like a new beginning—a new chapter in a story that had been filled with darkness and pain, but was finally moving toward the light.

"You should get some rest," Ms. Lawson said gently. "It's been a long night, and there's still a lot of work ahead of us. But for now, you've earned some peace."

Emily nodded, though she wasn't sure she'd be able to sleep. Her mind was still racing, her heart still heavy with everything that had happened. But as she followed Ms. Lawson toward the cabin, she knew she needed to recharge. There would be more battles ahead, more challenges to face, but for now, they had won a crucial victory.

As they stepped inside the cabin, Emily glanced back one last time at the forest behind them, her thoughts drifting to

Sarah. She wondered if, somewhere, Sarah's spirit could see the world waking up to the truth, see the people rallying against the injustice they had exposed.

She hoped Sarah knew that her sacrifice had meant something—that it had changed the world.

The door closed behind her, and for the first time in what felt like an eternity, Emily allowed herself to feel something other than fear and grief.

She felt hope.

It wasn't over yet—there was still work to be done, still battles to fight—but for the first time, Emily believed that they could win. The Satori Foundation had fallen, and in its place, something new could grow. Something better.

A new beginning.

Printed by Libri Plureos GmbH in Hamburg, Germany